WERE RAGES

WERE RAGES

WEREWITCH™ BOOK FIVE

RENÉE JAGGÉR

LMBPN Publishing
PMB 196, 2540 South Maryland Pkwy
Las Vegas, NV 89109

First US Release, September 2020
eBook ISBN: 978-1-64971-160-1
Print ISBN: 978-1-64971-161-8

CHAPTER ONE

The young woman, almost twenty-five years old, sat at the crude wooden table within the cabin, watching the sun go down over the mountains through the window. The day's fading light had turned blood-red as it fell over the little town of Greenhearth, Oregon, and it was all too easy to remember the people who'd been killed or wounded there in last week's battle.

So, she thought, *I officially became a were-shaman's apprentice—finally. I'm on the path now; it's real. I learned to control the magic powers I didn't even know I had a couple of months ago, so my abilities don't kill me. While I was at it, I pissed off a goddamn zealot cult of super-powerful, fanatical witches—our friends from the EU, the Venatori. And to deal with that crap, I built a loyal following of werewolf packs who've pledged to act as my army, and we kicked sorceress ass together. But they'll probably be back. Any week, any day, maybe any minute. They hated the werewolves before they hated me, so they get a twofer when they go after me.*

The man in the other room pulled the teakettle off a stove as it whistled, pouring the hot water into two cups.

Most girls, her mind plowed on, *spend their summers soaking up the sun in Cancun, learning just enough Spanish to know what "cerveza" means and flirting with dumbasses in tight swimming trunks. And here I am, preparing for a war. Oops?*

The man's heavy footsteps moved into the cabin's small, homey kitchen. He held a steaming mug in each hand. "Bailey. Your tea." His voice was deep and gruff, yet somehow calm. He set a cup down in front of her on the table, then sat down across from her.

Their meal was already on plates before them. Simple, but nice enough. Slow-cooked Salisbury steak, boiled peas, and mashed potatoes with real butter and homemade brown gravy. Just the kind of thing Bailey Nordin liked; it was good to find out that her mentor knew how to cook.

They ate in silence at first and waited till the meals were half-gone before they tried their tea, which had been served only a hair short of boiling. The sun set all the way behind the Cascades, and now the only light came from a small lantern on the windowsill.

Bailey sat back, taking a short break from her food. "This is kinda nice," she quipped. "The food, I mean, but also the cabin and the isolation. We can keep an eye on the town, but at the same time, we're far from it, and nothing down there can bother us."

Days ago, Greenhearth had been transformed into a war zone, and that was after weeks of buildup and increasingly strange occurrences. She'd decided she needed a short vacation, and her mentor had agreed.

"Yes," said Marcus. "I discovered this cabin in my wanderings over the mountains, and then I found it was for rent."

Bailey didn't ask how he'd managed to produce the money for that. Much of the time, she still thought of him as Marcus the local shaman, a tall, gruff, mysterious man who had befriended her when she most needed a teacher.

More and more, she found herself remembering who he really was—Fenris, a Norse god, the mythological father of the entire lycanthrope race. And he had chosen *her* as his apprentice.

"I'm glad," she affirmed. "As well as people seem to like me now, and even though I'm already kinda missing Roland, things were getting so crazy that there would be no way to focus on my training. Though I guess if the witches attack again, I won't have much choice.

The shaman nodded. "I'm proud of you. You've done well despite the short time we've had and all the pressure you've been under. But it's not over yet."

That was exactly what she'd expected him to say.

"You know," he went on, "that I can't intervene directly in the affairs that are unfolding in your town. Despite my non-interference, your growing power—and display of that power—has been attracting the notice of the other deities. Not only of my pantheon but of others. The gods are watching you."

The girl slowly sipped her tea as she ruminated, conflicted. She wasn't shocked; two of Fenris' extended family among the Aesir and Vanir had already made a pair of appearances. Specifically, Freya and Baldur had both shown up at unexpected times.

She set down her cup. "I've been training under you for a while, and I feel like I'm starting to get to know you. But still, there are times when you talk in a way where I can't tell what you mean. 'The gods are watching me.' Is that a good thing or a bad thing?"

It came out snappier and more insolent-sounding than she'd intended.

The tall shaman's inscrutable face shifted into a slight frown. "Both. It will depend on how they react, and what else happens on earth. It is a *serious* thing, no matter what else. We must be cautious."

She grimaced and looked out the window at the rolling slopes of the mountain below her, the topography gradually working its way down to Greenhearth.

Marcus continued, "Power attracts attention, and the greater the power, the more attention. It was inevitable that the higher powers would start taking notice. In the meantime, there's a more pressing concern. I don't think our feud with the Venatori is over yet."

"Neither do I," she admitted. "You'd imagine they would've learned their lesson. But at least we proved that we can beat 'em. I don't think they'll stop coming after me or werewolves, though, since they seem to hate both."

"Yes." The shaman gathered her cup close to him, as though preparing to take away the dishes, but he didn't get up yet. "Even if you don't press your advantage and take the fight to them, they will resent the bloody nose you gave them. They're in too deep. They've committed so much to trying to wipe you out that revenge is now an imperative for them to save face with their low-ranking members and affiliates if nothing else. They can't be seen as weak in front of global witchdom. A wound to their pride must be redressed. And they've always wanted to wipe out the werewolves. They've hated us from the time they formed, and werewitches in particular. I can understand them hating magic-users as a challenge to their dominance, but I don't know why they so loathe werewolves. Maybe they're trying to wipe out the race so we can't produce more were-witches."

Bailey swiped a hand through the air, annoyed with the thought of having to deal with them again. "Well, they're the ones who started the whole mess. They didn't have to invade my country and start killing my people. We never did a goddamn thing to them. Anyway, in the meantime, we've become stronger and more united."

It was true. Since the order of sorceresses had begun their elimination campaign against the Weres of the Pacific Northwest, more packs had declared allegiance to the prospective new High Shaman, Bailey. Those who hadn't come in person had sent word, or in some cases, donated a warrior or two to the defense of the Hearth Valley, under-standably keeping the rest to protect their own communities.

"We're ready for them this time," the girl said, allowing a note of grim satisfaction into her voice. "They're not gonna ambush a helpless settlement and burn it to the ground before anyone has the chance to fight back. Not now, or ever again."

Marcus stacked their plates and put the empty mugs and dirtied utensils on top of them. "It's good that the werewolves are now more vigilant, but do not get cocky or complacent. The Venatori have powers at their disposal beyond what you're aware of. They were able to teleport directly into town, bypassing the sentries around the rim of the valley."

"They won't get away with that shit again," Bailey snapped. She was tired of talking about witches. She'd rather focus on her training, the path to a future as a respected shaman. It freed her from the traditional obligation to marry before her twenty-fifth birthday.

Which wasn't far off. The reminder that she'd barely escaped that fate almost overwhelmed her with joy and relief.

Sensing her need to focus on her studies and progress further, Fenris did not push her. Instead, he picked up the pile of dishes and carried it over to the sink. "Relax," he told her, "and in the morning, we'll begin your training again—free from outside influences, at least for these few days."

"Sounds good to me." She beamed. Not having anything to do bored the shit out of her, but lately, there'd been too damn much.

Women converged on a beautiful centuries-old house that was cleverly hidden within the sprawling expanse of Lyon, France. It was one of two major edifices on the property owned by the Venatori.

Normally, meetings of the ruling council were held on the top floor of the Order's office building, but today they had extra guests. The ancient laws of hospitality therefore demanded they move the event to the mansion a half-kilometer south of the modern structure, which was far more comfortable and traditional.

From all over Europe, and even from America, witches had come to eastern France. Not only high-ranking members of the Venatori but also the leading lights of allied and affiliate organizations and hedge covens whom the Grandmistress felt might be sympathetic to their causes. There had not been any no-shows.

Once everyone was seated, the mansion's attendants took their drink orders, hastily bringing them silver goblets filled with excellent French wine. The Order had an entire cellar's worth, and the guests were allowed to pick their poison from among a selection of seven bottles. Not the very best, but good enough for a major occasion.

The servants bowed and excused themselves as the women finished their first draughts. Then the Grandmistress, Madame Daria Gregorovia, opened the day's discussion.

"Welcome," she intoned, "members, friends, and concerned parties all. Most of you have been here before. Those who have not, we hope you find our accommodations to your liking."

The private dining room within the mansion was half the size of a modern corporate conference chamber, with a vaulted ceiling rising seven meters over their heads. The stone walls were hung with tapestries of burgundy velvet embroidered with silver thread. A massive fireplace lay at the rear of the hall behind the Grandmistress, though given the relative warmth of the late-spring weather, no blaze had been lit.

"The affairs we discuss today," Gregorovia extrapolated,

"are a matter of concern to all sorceresses in Europe, in America, and indeed throughout the world. That is why we have invited so many of you from a variety of different places. As you may know, our ruling council has representatives from France, Belgium, the Netherlands, Ireland, the United Kingdom, Italy, Croatia, and Russia."

The council members raised their hands in greeting toward the others.

The Grandmistress resumed her speech. "Therefore, let us welcome those of you who are new here, having come on behalf of your countries. We particularly welcome Ms. Spages from the United States, even if her hometown in—is it New Jersey?—is far from that of Nordin in Oregon."

Spages frowned. "Yes, Madame. New Jersey."

"Good." Gregorovia paused for a sip of wine, exerting petty dominance over the assembled witches by forcing them to wait for her.

Unfortunately, Spages took the opportunity to speak up.

"I take it this has something to do with the psychopathic behavior of the witch who led your expedition in the Pacific Northwest? Even that obscure government agency of ours, who usually keep a lid on these sorts of things, couldn't keep that disaster out of the news. Discussion of the incident was all over social media. Of course, most people thought it was a gang war, terrorist attack, or false flag operation of some sort, but still, it attracted far too much attention. It certainly gave the werewolves a cause to rally around."

Her face indicated that she expected an apology.

Gregorovia waved a long-nailed hand. "It is true, yes,

that MacLachlan acted in a hasty, foolish, and excessive manner. That is why, as you look around this chamber, you will not see her here today. She has been removed from the ruling council and is ineligible for reentry for two years. As we speak, she performs penance duties. Due to her great skill at combat, we will retain her as a member, but she will not have any decision-making capability to speak of until she proves herself capable of restraint."

Spages shut up, and a round of gentle nods passed among the witches. Some clearly felt that more punishment was in order, but they seemed appeased by the knowledge that MacLachlan had at least been removed from command of the American expedition.

As a replacement duty, she'd been instructed to prepare and bolster the Order's defenses here in Lyon, getting the home guard in proper condition to resist a possible intercontinental attack by the American wolves. It was fitting, Gregorovia felt, for the Scotswoman to be placed in charge of dealing with the potential consequences of her actions.

"However," the Grandmistress went on, "Madame MacLachlan was correct in one important way. She foresaw that conflict with the lycanthropes was inevitable. We have all been resisting this obvious truth, but true it is. We have centuries of proof to show us that."

Half the witches shifted uncomfortably in their seats. Madame Dorleac, the council's second in command, looked ready to speak out in protest. The lone sorceress from the United States was also on the verge of argument. Perhaps, the Grandmistress thought, she feared an expansion of the violence on her home soil.

She preempted them by quickly resuming her spiel.

"The female werewitch is an abomination. It has been so long since one was born that we had forgotten the danger they posed, but Bailey Nordin has proven that a dormant threat is not the same as an extinct one. As long as the lycanthropic bloodlines are *capable* of producing such people, they are our natural rivals, and rivals must always eventually clash."

The malcontents appeared to think her words over. She'd reframed the issue such that the discussion would turn to the power of werewitches rather than the judgment of MacLachlan—or, for that matter, the judgment of Gregorovia in sending her.

"The Nordin girl," the Grandmistress explained, "continues to grow in power, showing a potential comparable to the greatest among us. She is young, ignorant, and inexperienced, but her raw strength is staggering. We have been unable to confirm for certain that she is being mentored by the god Fenris, but that possibility is not off the table. The best-case scenario has her under the instruction of a highly talented shaman."

Their guests, those who weren't members of the council, looked appropriately shocked at the suggestion of a deity intervening to guide and empower a mortal. They were ready for the last phase of Gregorovia's spiel.

"And," she concluded, "the girl has rallied wolves from all over the region, with word spreading across the entire American continent. Combine that with the allies she's made among humans, and soon she will have an army."

The unease that spread among the assembled channelers was like the change in the electrical charge of the air just before a thunderstorm.

Madame Iveta Smetanová, head of the Venatori's chapter in Prague, Czechia, clapped both of her hands to the table and looked around with wide, intense eyes. "The lycanthropes will not forget what we did on their home soil, and they have the Agency helping them. What happens if they decide to strike back at us in *our* homelands?"

Murmurs went around the table.

Madame Dorleac raised a hand. "We may be able to de-escalate yet, but it would be foolish to count upon it. Werewolves are not reasonable creatures. At a minimum, we should marshal our forces for defensive purposes and deploy reconnaissance units to America."

The Grandmistress agreed at once. "Yes, that is the plan I had in mind, though I wish to know that everyone supports our decision."

Some few of the assembled witches still seemed uneasy with the situation, but none outright objected.

"Ms. Spages," Gregorovia added, "is this plan agreeable to you?"

Spages was not a member of the Order, but rather the leader of a coven that claimed descent from the Old World witchcraft traditions and had been in friendly communication with the Venatori for the last three decades.

"It is," she began, "provided I have your assurance that we won't be dragged into a war of annihilation when a simple rebuke for any aggressive behavior on the lycanthropes' part would probably suffice. It's encouraging that MacLachlan is out of the picture, but if my coven is to cooperate, we must feel that we can trust the witches in charge of any further expeditions."

The Grandmistress promised the American that everything would be handled prudently.

The conference proceeded for another hour as the various enchantresses discussed the details. It then trailed off into more pleasant conversation, gossip, and casual talk of the practice of magic. The male attendants reappeared to refill their wine goblets.

Finally the guests were dismissed to their quarters, everyone in firm agreement that the Venatori and their allies must prepare for war and dispatch scouts to the United States, but should also avoid provocation.

At length, the only two women remaining in the great dining hall were Gregorovia and Dorleac.

"Grandmistress," the latter enquired, "was it your plan all along that MacLachlan would accelerate things so quickly?"

The other woman frowned. "No, not quite. I suspected we might be drawn into battle against those brutes, but not before we'd had more time to plan our strategy. But what's done is done. We are at war already, and I intend to win. Pay no heed to the hesitancy of our so-called friends. Our agents will strike swiftly and mercilessly, but in ways that will foment conflict between the wolves. With stealth and deception, we shall weaken their ties to one another—and the American governmental forces—before our witches sweep in to finish them off."

Dorleac smiled. "How...devious."

"Such is the way of things," the Order's leader stated. "For all our power, the raw physical strength of the lycanthropes, combined with the Agency's technology, paints a grim picture for us unless we can gain some advantage.

And I have other plans in mind, Madame, which I will not tell even to you. Not yet."

Her second-in-command settled back in her seat, her smile fading to an expression of mixed curiosity and jaded cynicism. "Well, then. I look forward to seeing the results."

Agent Townsend let out a deep, rattling sigh as he stared blankly at the screen of his monitor through the dark lenses of his glasses. Things had been far more interesting lately, insofar as he and his fellow agents had been able to strike back against the enemy.

But one thing still held true, regardless of how much the circumstances had changed—the more shit happened, the more shit had to be punched into his computer for analysis. And then, horror of horrors, the more shit had to be documented on reams upon reams of fucking paperwork.

"Bailey, Bailey, Bailey," he muttered, his chin resting on his chest. "Where is this going to lead? It's not your fault, but *damn!*"

The Agency still did not know the exact location of the Venatori's headquarters, nor had they been able to hack into their computer systems. Both were protected by extremely powerful magic. But they knew the Order was based in Lyon, and they had enough eyes and ears there to track increases in supernatural activity.

Especially when facial recognition software turned up individuals who were previously known to Townsend and his superiors paying mysterious visits to east-central France.

"Our lovely ladies are up to something," he grumbled. "Oh, Spall, where the hell are you, man? You're supposed to be here, offering your crusty-ass commentary on the whole situation. Well, at least you got your vacation."

Spall had been his partner for over a decade. All that was left of him now was a tiny pile of ash, courtesy of the European sorceresses. Spall's own recklessness *had* played a part, though. There was no denying it.

"You'd probably just say we know they're up to no good and that we should kick the shit out of them, blah blah blah," Townsend went on. "We did that. Last week. Got some payback on your behalf, my friend. Rest easy, wherever you are."

The computer still wasn't done crunching the numbers on all the data they'd collated. It might be another miserable half-hour.

The Agency already knew the Order was on the warpath. They'd helped repel the recent attack on Greenhearth, losing half a dozen men in the process, but killing more witches and sending their genocidal task force fleeing, tails between legs. It was hardly shocking to learn that the Venatori were plotting their next move.

There was also the matter of the prisoners they'd taken after the battle. Most had found ways to commit suicide before they could be properly questioned, much to Townsend's chagrin. The two who still survived were currently being held in tubes on life support, subject to another week of sensory deprivation. That ought to soften them up for interrogation.

Townsend knew the Order would be back, no matter what. Guaranteed.

Far more troubling was the revelation that the American shifters were growing more agitated. Much of this had to do with the Goddess of Shitstorms, Bailey Nordin. News and gossip pertaining to her rise and all the crap she'd been involved with were sending ripples throughout the proverbial pond. Some werewolves seemed less happy about it than others.

Most supported her, of course, and thought she was a hero. But the Agency's little birds had picked up a smattering of hostile chatter, too.

Some alphas thought she was aiming to become the Attila the Hun of Weres and weren't about to give up any part of their authority to her. Other packs were scared of retaliation (whether by the Venatori, the government, or society in general) and felt she was an uppity troublemaker.

And of course, Townsend and the Agency would have to deal with *all* of it, one way or another.

He prodded his monitor. "Don't hurry or anything. It's not like I have better things to do, like getting back into the fray and kicking witch ass. For fuck's sake!"

The computer responded by continuing to flash numbers at imperceptible speeds. At least the "Analysis Complete" progress bar grew a little longer.

Sighing, the agent turned back to his paperwork. All ten pounds of it.

CHAPTER TWO

Bailey had spent two days at the cabin. She and Marcus had been through a number of exercises, mostly meditation, breathing, and channeling activities that would help her manage her magic more efficiently. She felt It was useful stuff to practice, but somehow she'd expected to be learning or doing things that were on a whole new level relative to her current knowledge.

Otherwise, they passed their time relaxing in the forest and feeling its pulse, shifting to run along the crests of the mountains, and performing basic household tasks, all of which served to relax and energize her.

But she knew something was coming.

On the third day, after they'd had their morning tea and breakfast, Fenris instructed Bailey to go outside and wait for him on the ridge above the cabin while he cleaned up. She obeyed without a word.

Minutes later, the tall hooded figure strode out of the little house and moved up toward her. A hypnotic gravity of intent emanated off his powerful frame.

This is it, she realized. *Today is the day when my training as a full apprentice begins.*

Her mentor towered over her, silhouetted against the rising sun.

"Bailey," he began, "it is time for you to come to a full understanding of the burden of shamanhood. You've learned how to control your magic, how to fight, and how to be seen as a leader among your people. But there is more than that. You must also understand the *tradition* into which you're entering. You need to see that you'll be following in footsteps that reach back into history, long, long years beyond mortal counting."

She gave a tentative nod. "Okay. I'm ready for anything. And to be honest, I always wondered how old some of this stuff is. Weres have been around forever, it seems, but most people I know just have this vague idea that things have 'always been done' that way. No one seems to know how long 'always' means."

Fenris responded with a smile that was almost rueful. "It's easy for people to forget the depth of their customs when they feel they can take them for granted. But after what I'm about to put you through, that will no longer be the case. We're going to return to the Other and go some-place you haven't been before. A location that is sacred to our people."

Her curiosity flared from a twinkle to a roaring flame. No one had ever mentioned anything like that to her before. When people did talk about the ancient traditions of werewolves, it was usually in the context of their marriage laws, which, until mere weeks ago, had always left a sour taste in her mouth.

Now, at least, she was free of the obligation to be mated to a random alpha or one of his henchmen. With that burden off her shoulders, she was allowed to feel at home among her own kind.

Marcus plowed ahead, priming her for what she could expect. "This place is unique, a sort of otherworld nexus of residual memories, mental and emotional images, and what modern people might call 'team spirit' or 'group identity.' Where we're going, the past and the present blend in a timeless and interconnected pattern."

She furrowed her brow. "That makes sense, kinda."

"At least one pack of Weres must accompany you," he continued. "Once you're there, you will be required to lead them through a series of trials and challenges. It will not be easy, but you can do it. Upon completion, you'll be able to commune with the spirits of other shamans from the past. They will provide you with guidance, as I do in the present."

The god in human form had grown larger and darker than usual, yet his demeanor was not threatening.

"You'll learn who they were, where they came from, and what feats and deeds they accomplished, as well as the prosaic, day-to-day tasks they performed—a full account of their profession. They will instruct you in what they believe, and their feelings as to what a proper shaman's duties are. You'll find out how they died, and if their death was violent or otherwise unnatural."

She steeled herself. The visions she'd confronted in the Other before, whether they came from the black pool or courtesy of the hallucinogenic drink that transported her consciousness to the spirit world, had been terrible enough that she knew she could handle whatever came her way.

Fenris tilted his head so his gleaming eyes were visible beneath the hood. "You'll have access to all the advice that can be given and all the history that can be taught. Not only of werewolves, but also of witches, and the relations between our two peoples. And other wars, conflicts, relationships, and times of peace and plenty. The knowledge of all these things will serve you well on your journey."

She closed her eyes and gave a single slow nod. "I accept. I have to ask, though, what will happen with everyone else while I'm gone? It sounds like it could take a while, even with the time-distortion in the Other. And what about Roland? Can I take him along?"

Her mentor waggled a hand in an oddly irritable and undignified way. "You can bring him into the Other, but not into the trials. The place is dedicated to werekind. Intrusion by a member of witchkind would violate a number of primeval ordinances, and it's far better not to have to deal with those."

"All right," she agreed, shifting mental gears toward the fortitude she was certain she'd need. "We leaving right now, or can I have lunch first? Seems like my vacation is just about done at this point anyway."

He almost smiled. "Meet me back here at dusk with a complement of braves. Choose them or accept volunteers if they're willing. And Roland."

Roland stood in a small natural grove in the forest east of Greenhearth. It was in a flatter area, not quite into the foothills, and about a half-hour's walk from the center of town. The woods were dense enough to hide him from easy sight, and the location was a ways from the areas that had been devastated by the fights with the Venatori.

"Easy," he breathed, slowly moving his hands and repositioning his chest and hips. His eyes were closed. "Nice and easy. Flow and continuity. Communion and interconnection. All that good stuff."

He might have blushed if anyone could see or hear him, but what he did scarcely differed from a martial arts kata or certain religious practices. Its effects overlapped with both of those activities.

Basically, he was working out. Flexing his arcane muscles.

In time with a deep, slow, relaxed breath, he conjured a magical shield, one that flowed like water rather than remaining immovable and was virtually invisible. Its only visual cue was a shimmering ripple in the air, a distortion like that made by heat or vapor.

Usually, his shields glowed a faint emerald hue. One that was colorless might be more useful since attackers might not even know he was protecting himself.

The fluid barrier wrapped around him and spiraled upward as though he were at the center of an unseen tornado or whirlpool. Still inhaling and exhaling, and sensing the dimensions of the forest around him rather than looking at them, he maintained the spell as long as he could while gradually diverting some of his energy toward other pursuits.

The shield held as he charged the air around it with electromagnetic suffusions. Within the cyclonic barrier, a wind picked up and blew his blond hair away from his face in a spiky yellowish mass like a crown above his slender frame. Outside the shield, lightning bolts appeared in horizontal or curving patterns. The transparent whirlwind was both defensive and offensive.

After almost ten minutes, he dismissed the spell. The winds calmed, and the crackling electricity faded.

He leaned back against a tree, resting. Any good workout required a recovery period. In another ten minutes or so, it would be back to channeling in creative ways and summoning new effects. Exercising his magical will would increase his potential and limber up his range of abilities.

More and more, he was beginning to suspect that Bailey's potential exceeded his. She didn't have the years of experience he did, but while he was an abnormally gifted wizard, she seemed capable of truly astounding levels of raw power.

Roland coughed. "In any event, let's get back to it." He stood up straight, raised his arms, and opened his mind.

As he swept his consciousness over the hillside, seeking currents of subtle magic that he could weave into a sorcerous pattern, he detected a dead spot—a muffled location, barren of any magic whatsoever. That was both unusual and unnatural, not to mention familiar. It meant someone was cloaking.

He looked straight at the spot. The people under the arcane cloak must have known they'd been discovered since they cast it off. Revealed were three women in distinctive leather outfits somewhat like stylish, albeit odd, women's clothes mated with armor.

Roland's eyes flew all the way open and he raised his hands, prepared to shield himself while hammering the witches with offensive magic.

"Wait," the one at the lead said, holding up an opened palm in the universal gesture of non-aggression. "We are not here to harm you or fight. We only wish to talk. The Order does not know we are doing this."

Her accent was Spanish or perhaps Portuguese, Roland guessed, and his intuition said she was telling the truth. Clearly the woman was the leader of the trio, so the other two likely agreed.

"Talk, eh?" he quipped. "I'd say we have a *lot* to talk about after what happened."

The woman frowned; one might say *pouted*. "Yes, and we wish to apologize. That should never have happened. We were very sorry to hear about it."

The wizard was flabbergasted. Of everything they could have said, an apology was among the things he'd least expected.

It took a second or so for his mind to recover, then he returned to scanning the surrounding area, in case this was a devious trap. The witches might be trying to distract him while friends of theirs hidden nearby stabbed him in the back.

But there didn't seem to be any other magical presence in the woods.

"Uh, well," he drawled, "I'm glad to hear that, I suppose. I, too, am sorry that all this has happened."

It was a good neutral response. It indicated he was

willing to parlay with them, but he wasn't admitting any fault or groveling.

"Yes," the Spaniard riposted, "this has all been most terrible. I am Madame Villalobos, and I offer my forgiveness for the altercations of the past. That includes the one in which Madame Lavonne was killed. She was very respected. We apologize, nonetheless."

Roland tried not to frown. The woman's apology was taking on a rather odd note.

"And also," Villalobos went on, "we will forgive you for your involvement with Bailey Nordin and the lycanthropes."

At that, the wizard's teeth clamped together. He almost wished the sorceresses *had* attacked him just so he could kick their asses. He restrained himself, though, by prolonging the conversation. He might be able to learn more about their current plans.

The witch to the left of the leader spoke in a French or Belgian accent. "You are one of us. We don't wish to kill you. Please accept our offer of clemency."

Villalobos smiled. "You have our word about this. You have great power and potential, Roland, and we hate to see that wasted. Stand down and back out of the way before the Venatori come in full force. There is no avoiding conflict between our kind and Bailey and the shifters. You must choose a side. Not only for your sake, but for witchkind."

Roland folded his hands behind his back to hide their furious trembling.

"Because," the witch continued, "there is always the possibility that you will be corrupted by her power. Or that she, maddened with anger and hubris, will seek to strike back at all witches, making no distinction. Do you think she would choose you instead of her family and friends? And what about your family and your friends, back in Seattle? Do you think *they* will not be harmed by vengeful wolves?"

The wizard gave them the fakest, smarmiest smile his face was capable of.

"Gosh, sorry," he shot back, "but I'm afraid I'm going to have to ask you three ladies to *fuck off.*"

Their faces fell in perfect unison. Then all six of their eyes blazed with indignation and loathing.

Madame Villalobos' upper lip curled away from her teeth. "That is not how you talk to us when we have come in peace. We are making you a reasonable offer and giving you a chance to survive what is coming. How could you—"

"I will *not* leave Bailey's side," he interrupted her. "I appreciate you not trying to kill me. Really, I do. There's been far too much of that variety of bullshit in the last several weeks. But if you think I'm going to abandon the woman I love just because you issued a threat disguised as a peace offering, you're gravely mistaken."

Stiffening their postures and raising their noses in the air, the witches made ready to leave. "Have it your way," Villalobos sneered. She led her two minions away, their forms vanishing into the shadows of the forest.

Roland watched them go. He also tried to track them magically, but of course, they cloaked themselves, which made it impossible. He got the vague impression that they had transported somewhere far to the north.

Canada? he wondered. *That would make sense. Not*

terribly far, but out of the range of all the pissed-off Weres in Washington, not to mention outside the jurisdiction of the Agency. I'll have to mention this to Fenris and see what he says.

He no longer felt like training. He started to wander back toward his new home away from home—the Nordins' pole barn.

It had been weeks since he'd seen his family in Seattle. He'd called his mother and texted a couple of his old friends, assuring them he was all right, but that was it.

The words of the lead sorceress lingered in his mind. She had threatened his family. Oh, not directly. She might have just been trying to scare him with the half-assed possibility of the war spilling over and causing collateral damage, although that was scary enough.

If the Venatori sent a reprisal force against his kindred, though?

"I will *not* abandon Bailey," he told himself. If things settled down in Oregon, he might be able to slip north for a few days to check on them, but there was no way he would ditch her altogether. Not after all they'd done for each other, and everything they'd been through together.

Sighing and rubbing his face, he trudged through the woods. It was tough to say if he ought to keep walking to give himself more time to think or fly back so he could get a cup of coffee down his throat as soon as possible.

All four of the Nordin siblings had crowded into a booth in the rear corner of the Bristling Elk's diner wing. It had been far too long since Bailey had eaten out with her family.

Kurt was in a talkative mood. "So yeah, I think all the hubbub is affecting the track team's focus. We lost to those jerks from Estacada. How the goddamn hell does that happen?"

"Priorities." Russell grunted.

Jacob pursed his lips. "I guess so. You'd think getting pumped up for battle would make our guys, especially the Weres, faster, but I dunno. Track wasn't my thing."

Kurt poked him. "Little too much temptation around, am I right?"

"Shut up."

Bailey watched them talk and laughed here and there but didn't participate. She knew she was being borderline aloof. Her mind both drifted into the recent past and tried to charge ahead into the near future.

"Not gonna lie," she prefaced once there was a lull in the conversation, "I can't stop going over what might happen next with the Venatori and all. Gunney told me to take one thing at a time, and I suppose he's right."

Jacob shrugged. "He usually is. Anyway, the whole town is doing more than enough worrying, so it's not like you're obliged to do all of it yourself."

"True," she acceded and managed a half-smile.

Her eldest brother went on, "Besides, there's one particular noose that isn't looped around your neck anymore. Or your ass, I guess. Now that you're an official shaman's apprentice, it's a 'Do Not Touch' warning for all the eligible young gentlemen. The same old traditions that let them pressure you to mate mean they have to back off now."

All four of them smirked, savoring the irony.

"Yup." She sighed. "Damn. I don't think it's sunk in yet."

Ever since she'd hit puberty a good twelve years ago, the marriage requirement had hung over her head like the dangling sword in that old Greek legend. Then, a week ago, when Fenris proclaimed her his apprentice, it was simply *gone*.

Russell scratched his massive chin. "Kicking their asses doesn't seem to have convinced them to leave you alone. We'll see if ironclad customs do."

"They oughta," Kurt piped up. "Any sensible Were is gonna be more scared of his parents lecturing him about fucking up the family honor than he is of Bailey breaking his nose."

Jacob threw a playful punch at his younger brother, and Kurt deflected it just in time.

"Seriously, though," Jacob added, "there's still a handful of malcontents out there. Mostly the ones who don't believe Fenris himself chose you for the position. If we're lucky, they'll come around without us having to convince them in person."

Russell's hand clenched. "Convincing them might be kinda fun."

Ignoring the comment, Jacob went on, "Also, even though you're free of the *obligation* to mate, there's no rule that says you can't be, you know, wooed or courted or whatever like any other single woman. And of course, in addition to guys spreading the word that you're hot, being famous and important has a hotness all its own. Hate to say it, but you might start getting more attention from dudes than you used to."

She let her head fall backward and stared at the ceiling as she groaned. "Great. Juuuuust great…"

The announcement that she and Roland were an item was overdue.

Tomi, the usual waitress during lunch and dinner, approached with their sandwiches balanced on a massive tray. "Okay, guys, here you go. Russell, yours was the rare, right? And medium-rare for everyone else?"

"Yes," the middle brother rumbled.

She set the food down and told them to enjoy their meals, which they proceeded to do.

Bailey tore into her steak sandwich with an almost bestial hunger. Marcus had been keeping her well-sustained at the cabin with lean meat, vegetables, and other basic foods, and she was now craving something greasy and terrible. She'd have to prevail on her brothers to make chili mac or fried chicken later.

Soon the sandwiches had disappeared.

Jacob stretched his arms over his head. "I could use a drink."

"Me too," said Kurt at once. "Just pretend I'm new. Maury might not think to card me."

"Shit, "Jacob threw back, "that might be the single smartest idea you've ever had. It'll definitely work."

Bailey had to agree—with Jacob's suggestion, not Kurt's. As Tomi returned to gather up their dishes, Bailey caught her attention. "Hey, Tomi. Sorry, but we're gonna drift over to the other side, I think. Could use something more to wash down the meal."

"Okay." The waitress shrugged.

They left her a cash tip on the table but took their bill

with them to the bar. A moment before they seated themselves on a row of stools, the doors opened behind them, and in sauntered Roland.

He stopped and blinked, seeing the quartet. "Huh, they'll let anyone drink here nowadays. This town isn't what it used to be."

Bailey snorted. "Shut up, Seattle boy. Come have a beer with us, though."

"Not a bad idea," he acknowledged. "I was kinda thinking a cup of strong coffee, but a depressant might be just as comforting as a stimulant."

He joined them, selecting a stool to Bailey's left, and together, they took up most of the bar. Maury Fitzpatrick, the aging proprietor who usually ran the alcohol side of things during daylight hours, appeared from the back room.

"All of you together. That's a handful." He grunted. "What'll you have?"

"Beer," said Bailey. "Except for Kurt. Get him a Coke."

Nodding and sighing, the man went to bring their drinks.

The girl turned to the wizard. "So, what were you up to?"

"Practicing out in the woods," he answered her, "and thinking about, I dunno, what's next." He'd decided to keep the witches' visit to himself for now. Bailey didn't need to be told they were planning something else since she already knew it, and the rest would just hurt her feelings or worse, cause her to doubt him.

"Gotcha." She said no more than that. Roland's statement had a dual meaning, after all. The more obvious one was that he, like she, was worried about what might happen involving the Order and its vengeful agents, not to mention pack politics and so forth.

Less obviously, he probably meant what was next for *them* as a pair.

They'd finally gone all the way last week, and Bailey was overjoyed, in truth. Now they were *together* in every way that mattered. However, she hadn't told anyone except Gunney they were officially a couple. Her brothers weren't dunces, though; they must have suspected the possibility.

Maybe, Bailey considered, *Roland's hurt that I went off on a "vacation" with Fenris right after we did the deed. I'll have to tell him later it didn't have anything to do with him. I was just frickin' exhausted.*

The five chatted about minor stuff for a brief period before the doors parted again and a trio of young men, little more than teenagers, appeared.

"Hey," the one in the middle shouted, "are you Bailey Nordin?"

She wasn't sure she liked his tone. Then again, Weres weren't the most diplomatic people, and she'd already had a few come to pledge loyalty to her even when it hadn't seemed like that was their intent.

"Yup," she said, her tone casual as she turned on the stool. "You here to join the cause? If so, you're welcome to join us for a drink. Not sure you're old enough for a beer, but there's always soda."

"We ain't interested in a fuckin' drink."

All five of the seated figures turned to stare at the three kids. Examining them, their features as well as their clothes, and paying heed to their subtle smells and vibe, Bailey realized she'd been mistaken.

Only one of them, the one on the right, was a lycanthrope. The other two were humans. They dressed similarly, in nice but banal clothes that had been purchased recently and wouldn't have been much good out in the forest. The one in the lead had a baseball cap turned backward. Her visitors must have been from the suburbs of Portland or Salem, where lapsed Weres had gone native among the general population.

Maury waved a fat, hairy arm at them. "Hey, now. You boys don't have any business being here if you're not drinking or eating, or if you're only here to hassle my customers."

The one on the right made a faint jeering noise. The leader said, "Three Mountain Dews, then."

Frowning, the bartender went off to fish around in his cooler.

While he was gone, the out-of-towners came up behind Bailey and glared at her, unfazed by or not cognizant of the four large men she had with her. Not to mention her reputation for winning fights.

"So," the middle one began, "we heard you think you're the boss of all the Weres now, and that you're the fuckin' queen of Oregon or some shit. Dominic, is she the queen of the Weres?"

The one on the left, the domesticated lycanthrope, made a sputtering noise. "Hell, no."

"See," the leader went on, "Oregon City doesn't need your ass. It's got *us*, and nobody cuts in on our territory."

The Were chimed in with, "She does have a nice ass, though."

Roland looked like he was trying not to crack up. "Are you kids in a role-playing group? One of those D20 Modern things, where you're pretending to be in a gang?"

The middle guy's face snapped toward him. "Shut the *fuck* up. You look like a fashion model."

The wizard gestured with his elbow toward the dance floor. "Runway's over there if you want to see."

Bailey put one hand on her boyfriend's shoulder and extended her beverage in the other hand. "Hold my beer."

He accepted it from her and took a tiny sip from the bottle as he watched the werewitch and her new fan club stride toward the empty dance floor, in the wing of the building opposite the diner.

Maury gave him a cock-eyed look, gesturing toward the beer.

"What?" he asked with an innocent pout. "She's impossible to talk to some days until the hormones have worked themselves out or something like that. Besides, we all anticipate she'll need another one when she's done."

Jacob nodded. "True. You really do know her."

They watched as the fight began.

The young man who'd spoken for the group seemed to consider himself her primary opponent, but after a quick feint, Bailey ducked around him and went straight for his buddy the Were. The two crashed together with a sudden snarl of fury, then a hairy fist lashed out. Bailey ducked it to grab the boy and body-slam him into the wooden floor, kicking him hard in the gut for good measure.

Then the other two, both humans, piled into her. She staggered the leader with a sharp punch to the jaw, then took a blow to the stomach from the other guy before kneeing him in the groin and shoving him. He stumbled over his fallen friend and tumbled to the ground, clutching his family jewels.

"Hey!" the leader protested, remembering to bring his fists back up. "Bullshit! That's cheating!"

"What?" Bailey asked. "You didn't say anything about rules."

He started to charge at her, but she aimed a sidekick at his solar plexus, and his torso folded over her booted foot. Groaning and trying not to throw up, he slumped to his knees.

And that was it.

"Okay, then," Bailey stated, wiping her hands off on her jeans. She strolled back to the bar. "Gimme another beer, Maury. It looks like this dipshit drank a quarter of mine. Roland, I'm never trusting you to hold anything of mine again."

He whistled. "Harsh words. We'll see about that."

Moments later, as the three kids were dragging themselves off the dance floor, a sheriff's car pulled up outside, and Officer Smolinski strolled in. "Anybody dead?" he asked.

Russell looked at the deputy evenly. "No."

Nodding, the officer ambled over to the troublemakers. "Someone heard you boys bragging about how you were gonna take out the famous Ms. Nordin. You oughta at least keep your mouths shut in public if that's the kinda shit you plan to pull. You're all under arrest for disturbing the peace. And for your own protection."

"What?" the leader snapped. He turned his cap around the right way. "That's a bunch of crap. She hit us!"

"Yeah, yeah," Smolinski replied. "You have the right to remain silent…"

As he led the youths away, he paused beside the bar. "At least it's just normal shit this time, Bailey. Let's try to keep it that way, huh?"

She smiled.

Leading the trio away, he continued to admonish them. "You assholes could have stayed home, or maybe come here for the scenery and the outdoorsmanship stuff. But no, you had to go and pick a fight with Wonder Woman."

The five at the bar burst out laughing as the doors swung shut.

Jacob finished his beer. "Wonder Woman, my ass. Bailey's more a Marvel chick, I'd say."

"Nah," Kurt protested. "She's definitely DC. Just because the MCU movies made more money, it doesn't mean Marvel is better. Thanos is a complete rip-off of Darkseid. I mean, come on!"

Roland raised a finger. "Now that she's a werewitch, wouldn't that make her kind of like the bad guy from *Suicide Squad*? Only more, uh, physical, I guess."

"Horseshit," Jacob protested. "More like Storm from X-Men."

Bailey shrugged as she cracked open her second brew. "I'll take what I can get."

CHAPTER THREE

After a good meal and a brief if satisfying fight, there were still hours to kill before twilight. Granted, Bailey would need to find a wolf pack to accompany her to the trials Marcus had mentioned, but she doubted that would take long, with all the out-of-town Weres roaming around the valley.

After telling Roland about the trials, she ended up at the auto repair shop.

Gunney saw her coming and hailed her without looking up from his work. "Hi, Bailey. If you're looking for work, we got a whole bunch of shit to do on that Firebird, but that's gonna take a while, so there's also a basic oil change and maintenance check on this F-250 if you don't feel like challenging yourself."

She had to admit she didn't. "I'll take the oil change. I'm still a little tired and zoned-out."

"That works." He waved her over.

Gunney was a rather short but tough man in his early fifties. He was of an age with her father, and he'd fulfilled a similar role for much of her life. He had a scruffy beard and shaggy hair he usually kept hidden under a smudged old cap.

He and Bailey set to work on the Ford. Between the two of them, the job wouldn't take long, and it would be enough easy work to set her mind at ease and give them time to talk.

"So," she began, "after last week, I would've hoped the Venatori got the message—that they can't come around here killing and threatening us—and gave up and decided to stay home. Part of me wants revenge, yeah, but there's so much that could go wrong. I'd rather that fight was the end of it."

The mechanic nodded vaguely. He had a way of listening without looking at her, somewhat like he was distracted, but years of knowing him assured her that he was paying attention.

"But you don't think this will be the end," he surmised, finishing the statement for her.

She frowned. "Yeah. They have to save face after what happened. Or us fighting back convinced them we're an even bigger threat."

The girl relayed her other fears, admitting that she knew she ought to be focusing on the here-and-now, but with her increasing responsibilities, it was almost impossible.

All the while, they checked the F-250's brakes, rotors, and filters, opting to replace the latter, and topped off all the fluids, which didn't seem to be leaking.

They were nearly done when Bailey concluded with, "I

dunno if there's any way to stop the escalation at this point. Those witches have got to be hurting."

To her surprise, Gunney snorted with contempt. "Well, they oughta be. Fuck them."

Bailey had expected him to offer his usual sort of advice, stuff that was calming and reassuring, replete with analogies about how best to view the situation differently. Instead...

"They started this. They came after you and yours, and all the rest of us here besides. When was the last time Greenhearth, Oregon hurt or threatened anyone in goddamn France? If they never show up again and you decide to let bygones be bygones, fine. But if they have the nerve to come back here again, Greenhearth will kick their asses even harder. You've got an army of Weres now, plus, those government guys are on our side, and we all know what to expect. We're fighting to defend our homes, and that counts for something. If they're still looking for a fight, they'll lose. Believe it."

The way he said it, she no longer had any doubts.

"Shit, Gunney," she murmured. "You got a point there. Thanks. I think I needed to hear that."

"You did," he affirmed, "and I suppose I needed to say it. Makes *me* feel better, too."

They talked about a few more things—what color Bailey planned to paint her Camaro, what work would look like next week—until the sun grew low enough in the sky that Bailey recalled she needed to head up the mountain.

"I gotta go," she told the mechanic, shaking his callused

hand. "I'll record this on the timesheet, and I'll be back soon, I promise."

He smiled. "I know you will, girl. Take care of yourself."

She was walking back to her car, still matte gray and unfinished, when four figures approached. At the head of them was Will Waldsbach, the alpha of the South Cliff pack, who'd pledged themselves to her cause.

"Hi, Will. Guys," she greeted them.

Before she could ask if they'd be willing to volunteer for a field trip into the Other, Will spoke.

"Bailey. Roland sent us your way, saying you needed Weres to help you with some kind of magical trials. So, here we are."

She tried not to laugh at her good luck. "That works out perfectly since I'm on my way now. It's too far to walk in time, though, so why don't you guys head west on Main Street, and I'll pick you up in my truck? Just gotta drive home to get it."

The four nodded. "Deal."

Will grinned as they came to a stop. "Hell of a nice ride," he remarked.

"Thanks," said Bailey. "Would've expected to hear that compliment on my *other* car, but that thing wouldn't fit all you dumbasses."

One of Will's friends piped up, shouting through the rear window. "That's okay, you can take us out one after another in it when we get back."

Roland made a sour face at that, but the Weres all just laughed.

Bailey had brought the pack along in her Tundra, with Will in the passenger seat and Roland, due to his skinny frame, in the half-assed back seat. The other guys rode in the bed. They'd covered themselves with a tarp until they were out of town, since even though she had an understanding with Sheriff Browne, she would rather not risk a ticket.

Her other vehicle, of course, was a '72 Camaro—a gift from Gunney after she'd helped him restore it. *That* thing was too precious for an errand like this.

The six of them got out of the vehicle and stepped onto the dirt patch where the winding mountain road ended. The cabin Marcus had rented was about a quarter-mile up the footpath. As her boots struck the earth, Bailey hoped she'd brought along enough Weres. Marcus had said something about a full pack, she recalled.

Mere seconds after she'd had the thought, figures appeared on the path ahead. They were little more than black silhouettes in the dim reddish light of evening, but the one at the front wasn't hard to recognize with its height, broad shoulders, and hood.

"Bailey," said Fenris, "these young men came looking for you. They've just arrived from Washington, and they wanted to talk to you before the trials." He gestured to the other six forms, then stepped back to let them speak for themselves.

The werewitch stood where she was, with Roland and Will flanking her and the other three South Cliffs hovering nearby.

One man moved out in front to speak for the group. "My name is Roger Hathaway," he opened, in a voice that was higher-pitched than Bailey would have guessed, although he was still well-spoken and formidable-looking. "My father's the alpha of the Silver Star pack, and I'm in line to succeed him soon. We heard about what you been doing for Weres."

She nodded. Compliments like this were starting to become routine, and she had to work to stop them from going to her head. A real shaman didn't get drunk on power or celebrity. "Thank you, Roger. Where are you guys from in Washington?"

"Southern part of the state," he elaborated. "Not too far northeast of Portland. The Venatori wiped out our neighbors, but somehow they missed us. Almost feels like we were too lucky…and half of us have been lying awake at night, thinking how we should have heard them coming and done something to save that other pack, the Merwin Lakes. We want to make up for it by helping you."

Nods from the other five guys; the mood among them was serious but friendly.

"Okay," said Bailey. "Glad to hear it. Right this moment, what I need help with is a series of trials in the Other—you ever been there?—but that's asking a lot, so if you're not up for that, I'd say head on down to Greenhearth, ask around with the other Weres, and see what they say you can do. Or talk to the sheriff. He knows me, and he'll get you set up somewhere."

Roger huddled with his men, and they muttered among themselves. Bailey overheard enough to determine that they were trying to decide whether to accompany her into the alternate world.

Fenris said nothing. Bailey wondered if he'd already explained to them what they might expect, and they were simply waiting for her to ask.

After a minute or two, they split back into a loose cluster, and Roger took a deep breath. "We'll accompany you into the trials," he stated.

Bailey smiled gently. "You're brave, then. You didn't tell me if you have any experience with the Other. It's nothing to fuck around with."

"We've heard of it." Roger's jaw tightened. "The Merwin Lake pack died because we weren't able to come to their aid in time. We can take the risk. We came here because we heard you were leading all the wolves in the region in our mutual defense. Lead, and we'll follow."

It occurred to her that if she didn't set a good example by bringing them along and trusting their courage and ability, they might take it as an insult and question her judgment.

"Done," she said. "I'm glad to have you guys since the crew I have here at present isn't the biggest. Don't beat yourselves up too much over what happened. It was Venatori's fault, not yours, but I understand what you mean about feeling guilty. Just for volunteering, you've redeemed yourselves in my eyes."

It was hard to see, but it looked like the alpha's son swelled with pride at that. "Our god told us," he related, "that those who passed the trials would walk through the halls of our ancestors and the shamans from the past. We want to be known as the Weres who joined you for that."

Marcus stepped forth. "A dozen of you, then, and I make thirteen, although neither Roland nor I will be present for the trials. Now, then…"

He turned to an empty patch between trees, chanted, and then raised his arms, deep in meditation. At a swipe of his hand, a gateway opened in midair like a pool of liquid amethyst layered over a well of midnight purple-black. Half the Silver Stars drew sharp, sudden breaths.

Fenris glanced at the Weres and Roland. "Follow me." He stepped through and was gone.

Bailey had been about to lead the way, but Roger and his Weres beat her to it, as though impatient to prove themselves despite their surprise at seeing an interdimensional portal open for the first time. One by one, their burly forms vanished into the shimmering violet mass.

Roland coughed. "Well, if by some chance they're here to assassinate us on behalf of the Venatori, then at least Fenris can deal with them."

"They're not," Bailey insisted. "I know these are paranoid times, but have a little faith. I've heard of the Silver Star pack, although I never met them myself. Now, let's get this show on the road."

She strode forth, Roland, Will, and the others behind her, and in a few steps, they no longer stood on the soil of Earth.

The sensation was cold, tingling, and dizzying, but it only lasted a second. Then she stepped into the Other. She drew a breath as sharply as Roger's boys had.

Fenris had taken them to a part of the dimension she'd never seen before, and it was nothing like the rest. Most of the Other was a dark, chilly, desolate place composed mainly of swamp, rocks, and dead trees, with eerie silence under oppressive skies of deep purple and sheets of clouds the color of slate.

This corner of the arcane world was another story. Lush, brighter, and full of life, it awed her with its beauty.

Unending old-growth forest stretched in all directions across rolling ground carpeted with green grass and moss. These trees, unlike the ones Bailey had encountered before, were in full bloom, their roughly patterned limbs swaying under the weight of thousands of emerald leaves. Thick flowering vines wrapped around the trunks of one in every six or seven.

There was also a brilliant silver light. Looking up, Bailey saw a full moon directly overhead, seemingly ten times larger than the moon of Earth. The sky behind it was a deep blue-black like that of a summer night, yet the radiance was so powerful as to make it nearly as bright as day. Stars blazed and twinkled with light that shifted from white to gold to azure.

In the distance, wolves howled. There was a mysterious joy in them, totally different from the menace that people, even modern weres, associated with the sound.

Finally, the breeze was cool without being cold. It reminded her of both the gentle winds of summer that gave relief from the heat and the slight chilling of the air months later that indicated the arrival of autumn. When the breeze faded, wisps of mist rose from the plants.

Bailey was unable to move or speak for a moment. "This place is incredible. It's like a paradise."

She recalled that it was the destination of the spirits of were-shamans, apparently where they dwelled in eternity.

She was afraid to ask the next question, but she did regardless.

"Is this…" She swallowed. "Is this our heaven? The werewolf afterlife?"

Behind her, she heard the others fidget as their minds grappled with the notion.

Marcus turned toward her, his face solemn. "I cannot reply to that directly, but I will say that the answer is more complex than a simple yes or no. For the moment, there are things we need to do. Come, but walk. Do not run. And walk on two legs."

The tall shaman led the way through the enchanting primeval forest, leaving his people to wonder if, as their god, he had created this realm or made it his own home.

Roland broke the silence. "Why two legs, if I might ask?"

A couple of Weres made low grumbling sounds at the impertinent inquiry, but Fenris didn't seem bothered.

"Here," he explained, "no lycanthropes walk shifted through the woods until they reach the place where they must be. It is a rule, and not one we can break."

His matter-of-fact tone suggested that it would be useless to ask for further details. He'd stated a fact, comparable to the rising of the sun in the east back on Earth.

The thirteen figures continued their march for what felt like hours—in the Other, the passage of time was distorted—yet they didn't grow tired or feel any pangs of thirst or hunger.

Bailey sensed they were going slightly uphill. The omnipresent trees were less numerous, and the soft ground had more outcroppings of rock, which gleamed with a faint silvery sheen.

Furthermore, both trees and stones were inscribed with wolf faces, moons in various phases, and runes she didn't recognize. The sigils seemed to be pointing toward something.

They passed through a screen of tall leafy weeds growing between two massive green oaks, and suddenly they were in a clearing on a small plateau.

"That *must* be our destination. Right?" commented Will.

Fenris stopped. "It is."

In the center of the clearing rose a massive stone structure like a pyramid of steps or a ziggurat, towering approximately as high as the enormous trees of the surrounding forest. At each of its four corners was a wolf-headed totem made of the same dark gray rock. Silver fog surrounded the building on all sides.

Roland whistled. "Nice place. That's not normal mist, though. I'm guessing you have a plan to get us through?"

Marcus nodded. "Yes, but not you, Roland. You must remain here throughout the ordeal, no matter how much you might worry about Bailey. As a non-Were and a witch, your presence would disturb the sanctity of the place and raise the ire of the shamanic spirits who reside here. In their fury, they would attack anyone they saw, including Bailey. I cannot go, either. It's something she and her Weres need to do alone."

The girl and the wolves all nodded, having noted that the reply was meant for them as well as the wizard.

Fenris walked over to the glimmering mass of fog and placed his right hand on it as though it were a solid wall.

Then he bowed his head, and in a deep, almost gurgling voice intoned a chant in what may have been old Norse or some language even more ancient. Bailey couldn't understand any of it, but the strange words chilled her spine in a way that wasn't unpleasant.

The fog thinned and faded but did not vanish.

"Go," said Fenris. "I can't tell you what you'll face, but be brave and be honest. Good luck. I believe in you, Bailey, and I believe in the courage of all you others who have volunteered to be at her side. Now, go!"

Swallowing and breathing in through her nose, Bailey strode through the misty barrier, ten Weres filing through it behind her. The fog briefly slowed her and was shockingly cold, but the sensation passed instantly.

They stood before the gaping black entrance to the temple.

Bailey paused to address her followers, looking into their glinting eyes. "If we're uncertain, I want you to advise me on what's best. But if *I'm* certain, and I *tell* you what to do, you do it. Understand?"

They all nodded.

She walked straight into the darkness.

At first, it seemed the ziggurat's interior consisted of nothing but blackness, but after the first half-dozen footfalls, its interior took form. The structure was hollow, and soon they were descending a huge staircase of broad, shallow steps leading deep into the earth.

When their heads were level with the floor, the stairs wound to the side before depositing them into an underground hall or gallery where the light increased.

Torches produced a steady smokeless fire that gave off

silvery-white light like stars. They were affixed to thick stone columns that rose from the smooth floor to a point far above their heads. The walls spread for at least a hundred feet in either direction and were carved with friezes showing lupine forms in various stages of hunting.

The hall was filled with statues, each about twice the size of a human. Many had the forms of men, or occasionally women, dressed in flowing robes that were both primitive and formal. Others were in the shapes of wolves. It occurred to Bailey that the former probably represented important shamans, while the latter might have represented her people's primordial kinship with the beasts of the wild.

Everyone was silent as they filed slowly toward the center of the chamber. The place was like a tomb, and it seemed like noise would desecrate it.

Bluish-silver light coalesced in front of them, bringing them to a sharp halt. A vaguely humanoid form, bright and featureless, stood before them.

"*Who are you?*" it asked in a clear and echoing yet weirdly subdued voice. "*What is your purpose here?*"

Steeling herself, Bailey stepped forward to answer. "Bailey Nordin, of Greenhearth, also known as Nova. I'm an apprentice shaman to Fenris, father of all werewolves. He requested that I come here to learn more about the path to becoming High Shaman. I'm here with Weres who've pledged loyalty to me, and anything you have to teach us, we're willing to learn."

Silence, oppressive and total, hung in the air for a moment.

Then the spirit responded, "Being apprenticed to Fenris

will not save you if you are not ready, alert, and willing to do whatever must be done. We sense your sincerity and the truth of your words. But is your heart prepared for the first test?"

Before she could answer, the glowing spirit shifted into the far more detailed form of an enormous blue spectral wolf with eyes like blood moons. Then it pounced.

Bailey was already trying to react, somehow, and heard her followers cry out. The creature moved too fast even for her, and fear and confusion welled up as the ghostly form struck her in the chest, extinguishing the light and sending her reeling into total darkness.

CHAPTER FOUR

Jamie Gryphon and her friends Marcia and Elizabeth sat on a bench arranged near one of the lakes at the Nature Park in Newport News, Virginia. They talked.

"Ugh," Jamie opined. "At least they have like, *civilization* down here. *Kinda.*"

Her friends laughed. "I know," Marcia concurred. "Can you imagine if we'd broken down over there? I don't even want to think about it."

"Horror movie shit, for sure," said Elizabeth. "Wouldn't have been so bad if we could have shared a car instead of having to drive separately."

The three of them had taken a week off from their day jobs in Washington, DC, and spent the previous day scouting out lycanthrope settlements in West Virginia. It was the first time Jamie had set foot in the state, and her wingwomen had only driven through the wretched place.

Being in coastal Virginia was an improvement, though still vastly inferior to DC. Their guests ought to be arriving any minute, then they could leave.

51

They chatted for perhaps five more minutes before a rented bus pulled up on the nearby road, its brakes squeaking as it ground to a halt. After its doors opened, women dressed in nearly identical leather outfits stepped down one by one and crossed the grass toward the bench. There were a total of twenty-one of them.

Once all the passengers had vacated the vehicle, the short, wide lady who seemed to be in charge waved a hand at the driver. He nodded vacantly and drove off.

"Okay," Jamie muttered, breathing deeply and standing up. Marcia and Elizabeth did likewise as she addressed the group. "Hello. I saw those getups in a fashion show. Are you here for something like that?"

It was the agreed-upon code. The newcomers smiled and nodded, aside from the squat one, who pushed through the others to stand at the front.

"Something like that, yes," she replied in a slight French accent. "Do you girls know the best way to Lynchburg?"

Jamie bristled but tried not to show it. Their Venatori contact was supposed to say, "ladies," not "girls."

"Yeah," she agreed. "We can show you."

"Good." The short older woman smirked. "Let us go this way."

The entire crowd, two dozen strong, tramped across the green expanse to the out-of-the-way lot where Jamie, Marcia, and Elizabeth had parked their three vehicles, not to mention the extra three they'd rented. It was a motley assortment of sedans, SUVs, and minivans, but it would suffice to get them to West Virginia.

Once they were certain no one was watching or listening, the squat lady sidled up to Jamie. "I am Madame Chauvin," she stated, "and I am in command of this mission. You are Jamie Gryphon of the small coven we contacted from the District of Columbia?"

"Yes, but it's not that small. We have like, a full thirteen members now, but six of them are new and don't know what they're doing yet."

Chauvin nodded, walked past her without a word, and began directing her people to divide themselves into six groups—three trios and three quartets. The smaller groups would be rounded out by the American witches.

Jamie briefly reconvened with her friends. "This bitch clearly thinks we're just here to escort her or something," she growled. "Once the killing starts, I think she's going to get a surprise."

They all smiled. Their contacts in Europe had hinted at the possibility of Venatori membership for anyone who aided them. That was the goal.

After a brief discussion of who would be going to each settlement, they went their separate ways, two vehicles per target community. Jamie was unsurprised that Madame Chauvin divided the Americans up between the three groups and that she commandeered the other, a rented Ford SUV that would be accompanying Jamie's Camry to the cluster of cabins near Watoga State Park.

It was almost a five-hour drive. The idea was to arrive at or immediately after dark, but still, Jamie found herself wishing the werewolves lived closer to the coast or to places large enough to qualify as cities. But no, they had to live out in the boondocks.

The European witches ignored Jamie for the most part,

yammering in French and occasionally asking her banal questions while ignoring her inquiries.

She had information, though. Stuff that had come down through the grapevine, whether the Venatori meant to leak it or not. Most notably, that the Order had sent troops all over the United States, Canada, and Mexico, aided by sympathetic locals, to begin a coordinated series of strikes against werewolves across the continent. They'd had no trouble recruiting. In general, witches hated werewolves, even though they might not know why anymore. They were happy to join the great effort to eradicate the packs.

In the forests of New England and Quebec and the northern Great Lakes region, packs were being hunted down and destroyed. In the swamps of the Deep South, packs woke up to carnage, then never awoke again. On the windswept prairies of North Dakota and Saskatchewan, packs accustomed to freedom blundered into traps. In mountain hollows within the craggy deserts of West Texas and Chihuahua, packs looked up and saw death raining down on them.

Jamie and her friends would do their part. Appalachia, too, would soon be rid of the lycanthropic vermin and the threat to witchkind they represented.

Night had fallen when they arrived at their destination, a wooded area outside the little town of Hillsboro, West Virginia. Here a good dozen houses, radiating out for a half a mile from an intersection of two dirt roads, were all inhabited by werewolves.

As per the instructions, Jamie parked behind a tree just beyond the de facto hamlet. She and the three foreign witches stepped out, and the SUV containing Madame Chauvin pulled up a minute later.

The squat witch made a circular motion with her hand. "Surround these houses," she ordered, "and trap them all within a wall of fire which moves inwards."

Jamie drew in a breath and stepped into the forest, separated from the other seven by what seemed a too-long expanse to either side. She felt the power of the Venatori agents growing in her head, and she merged with the coven-mind they formed.

Oddly, part of the collective mind was blocked off from her. She'd never encountered that before; it must have been a side effect of the Venatori thinking in French, a language she didn't know.

Then a cue rang out, clear as an alarm bell. Once the fire had formed a complete circle, they released it and pushed it inward.

It swept across the land, scorched grass and trees, and turned the buildings into infernos before the circle closed entirely on the road intersection and then exploded in an immense fireball. Jamie shielded her eyes and ears from the effects of the blast, mildly frightened.

"Good, everyone," said Madame Chauvin. "Jamie Gryphon, stay where you are."

She was helpless to disobey, even though a sense of wrongness hit her in the gut when she realized the other seven sorceresses had fled the scene.

The betrayal was clear; a mass of shifted wolves, foaming at the mouth with rage, emerged from the forest across the street from where she stood and dashed straight toward her. She could fight, but she could not move from the spot where she stood, a victim of some magic beyond her ability to undo.

Desperately she conjured another wave of flame and sent it toward the Weres, engulfing two, but then the rest were upon her.

In making their initial strikes, the Venatori would leave their American accomplices to act as bait and take the fall. Jamie wounded one more wolf before the others tore her to pieces.

Madame Chauvin and her six underlings had piled back into the two vehicles and were speedily driving far away from the scene.

Southwest of there, near Bluestone Lake along the New River, a large-scale melee had been joined between the rest of the Venatori and their collaborators and those were-packs that had heard the rumors and come to help their fellows. The goal, Chauvin recalled, was to create as many American casualties as possible among both the lycan-thropes and the witches while preserving the lives of Order members.

That would rouse the werewolves and make it appear as though their species were going out of their way to attack local representatives of witchkind in a misguided form of retribution for the Venatori's campaign in the Pacific Northwest a couple weeks ago.

Bailey would *have* to fight, and all-out war could begin. At last.

As they drew closer, the lights of the battle began to illuminate the sky. The violence being unleashed there must have been incredible. Smiling and shuddering at once, the veteran sorceress doubted that achieving maximum death and destruction would be terribly difficult.

"Bitches," Townsend snarled. They now had visual confirmation that all four of the women within the supposedly abandoned Portland warehouse were dressed in standard Venatori uniforms.

The man to his left looked at him. "What do we do, sir?"

Townsend's jaw muscles rippled. "Move in and take 'em out, according to the procedure. As in, neutralize the threat, detain, and question first. If they're stupid enough to fight back, shoot to kill."

"Yes, sir."

He had seven men with him, all heavily armed and outfitted in paramilitary gear. They outnumbered the witches two to one, but even a single Venatori could be extremely dangerous if one wasn't careful.

Two agents remained outside on the earthen half-wall surrounding the lot, which was mostly covered by trees, acting as snipers in case any of the suspects tried to flee. The other six moved in on the building.

While Agent Sorvald, a newer and younger guy, planted a suspension-field mine at the front entrance, Townsend supervised the entry into the warehouse through the back door.

Predictably, they encountered multiple defensive runes.

"Okay." Agent Perez sighed as he moved the scanner over the walls. "There's an invisible one right beside the door—there. It's a silent alarm. Hits you with a psychic pang if you come too close to it."

Townsend nodded. "Of course. You know what to do, Perez."

The other agent fired up the scanner's built-in abrader beam—a narrow, intense, and colorless laser that would melt and deface magical sigils, rendering them useless. Tongues of flame leapt from the surface as the rune distorted and then was lost altogether in the half-liquefied material.

"Move in," ordered Townsend.

As they went through the motions of stealthily cutting the door open and slipping into the shadows within the building, Townsend reflected on why they were here.

The Venatori, unsurprisingly, had failed to learn their lesson, which was typical of fanatics. After the defeat of their main force in Greenhearth, they'd continued to slip in reinforcements, suggesting that they'd always meant to escalate the conflict but were simply lying low for a couple weeks until their next move.

When word had come in that a quartet of possible Venatori had been detected in Portland, Townsend had prioritized dealing with them over everything else. Portland was little more than an hour from Bailey's hometown. He'd insisted on leading the mission.

Within the warehouse was one more alarm rune. Perez neutralized it the same way he had the first, while another agent covered the slight heat-blaze with a small Vantablack screen, and a third used a mobile cloaking device to protect them from easy magical detection.

The group paused to examine their targets. The four

witches sat on two couches under a dim lamp, shuffling and looking at cards. It was impossible to say whether they were diverting themselves with a game or engaged in some kind of divination. Not that it mattered.

Townsend motioned for the man with the cloaking device to move to the far side of the warehouse to create a diagonal crossfire if the suspects resisted. Then Townsend and the other four walked into the central space, arcanoplasm guns held at the ready.

"Okay," Townsend barked. The women sprang to their feet instantly. "Hands up. Do not try anything, or you're dead. We're taking you in for questioning. You ladies understand English, right?"

To be safe, Agent Perez repeated the instructions in French.

Scowling, the witches slowly raised their hands. Then one threw a lightning bolt.

"No!" someone squawked. The bolt deflected off a portable shield as magenta beams streaked from the agents' guns. Two witches collapsed in sparking piles of ash as the other two bolted for the front door.

The one in front triggered the suspension-field mine. A purplish dome of light spread out, trapping her in place and incapacitating her with painful static shocks.

The fourth and final witch stopped a foot short of the magenta field and spun to face the agents. She was a tanned blonde woman who looked downright furious.

Townsend snapped, "Stop or you die. What were you doing here? *Tell us.*"

Obviously suppressing her urge to fight, the woman

swallowed and said in a heavy German accent, "We are here for Bailey. Unfinished business with her. That is all."

"Oh, really?" Townsend jeered. "Last time your organization came 'just' for Bailey, you ended up turning the Northwest into fuckin' Syria. Now, you and your friend there," he gestured with his chin toward the other witch, who was still trapped in the suspension field, "are going to come with us and tell us the truth."

Before the sorceress could respond, Agent Wilson came up to Townsend, holding aloft a cell phone on which he'd taken a call. "It's for you, boss."

Frowning, Townsend spoke into the receiver without taking his eyes off the blonde sorceress. "Townsend. What's up?"

"Agent," the voice intoned, "we have a major incident in Eastern. Three Were settlements in West Virginia were burned, followed by a god-awful pitched battle out in the hills. It looks like it was mostly local witches involved in the carnage, surprisingly. But between them and the wolves, the death toll is in the dozens and growing. Might pushing multiple hundreds. We need you back at HQ on the double to get on speakerphone with the agents who witnessed the scene."

The German witch suddenly shot straight up into the air, throwing a wave of boiling acid as she rose.

"Shit!" Sorvald exclaimed as half of the lethal substance blanketed his arm and side, raising steam from his black tactical armor.

The other agents fired arcane beams in a constricting pattern at the woman as she tried to crawl along and then through the ceiling. Just before she reached a skylight,

Townsend put a magenta ray through the back of her head. Her top half ceased to exist, and her burning bottom half plummeted toward the floor.

Two other agents were helping Sorvald strip off his armor. Beneath it, his skin was messed up, and he tried not to scream in pain. He'd need an ambulance, but he would live. Townsend called 911 at once.

Meanwhile, Agent Perez clapped a pair of anti-magic cuffs on the one remaining sorceress after the suspension field started to fade. The Agency was improving its suicide prevention measures. They'd probably get something useful out of the woman.

"Still," Townsend growled more to himself than to his men, "at this rate, we're going to have to start telling our guys to just shoot them on sight."

Bailey's eyes snapped open. Before her was an endless expanse of black, absolute nothingness without dimension or direction. It was at once flat and infinitely deep in its lack of features.

Only one thing was visible, directly in front of her: the blue spectral wolf who had pounced on her with such speed that she'd been unable to react.

Shouting reflexively, she brought up her arms, summoning a thick swath of electricity and arcane plasma, enough to block most incoming attacks while itself providing offense against the hostile spirit. She threw the crackling reddish mass at it.

Although it was blazing white, its light did nothing to

illuminate the darkness that was all around. After striking the air in front of the wolf, it fizzled away to a wisp of steam and was gone.

Bailey gaped, and the wolf looked at her with its steadily glowing eyes.

"Stop," it commanded in a voice much like the one she'd heard the spirit use in the temple, only gentler. "This is not an attack on you, but a private inquisition into your heart and soul. You are not here to defend yourself from physical harm."

She breathed out, dismissing the worst of the tension in her and trying to trust the spirit's words.

"Here and now, Bailey Nordin who is called Nova, your inner fears, private thoughts, and deepest, most secret desires will manifest—not for battle, but for discussion. You might find it more trying than combat, for your heart will be laid bare for the shamans who linger in this temple to see and judge. There shall not be unconditional acceptance. You must be worthy."

Hearing that, she quailed, then dispelled the fear with a short shake of her head. She nodded slowly in the dark.

"If you are false in your words or intentions, or if your intentions are mad, foolish, or grossly impure, it will go poorly for you. Thus it is not a test of skill or ability. This hall has seen many shamans of average talent who nevertheless were accepted because they meant well. Because they were willing to learn, grow, and compromise. Thus they were found worthy."

"Okay," she replied, wishing she had something cleverer to say.

"Now, Bailey," the wolf concluded, "we will learn. Deep down, are you doing this for the right reasons?"

In less time than it takes the eye to blink, the spirit was gone, and in its place was a circle of men around the girl's position. She didn't know any of them personally but recognized their type. Each of them was a pack alpha, strong and true to the ways of wolfdom but of a greedy, unimaginative, often cruel type. They looked at her the way they might view a side of meat when hungry.

Their hands reached out to grab her, clutching her clothes, the flesh of her bare arms, or the curve of her hips, all trying to pull her toward them. Struggling not to panic, she fought them off, ripping herself free of their grasp, swatting away their hands, moving into what little space she could make by force between them. She didn't let any of them touch her for more than a second.

She was terrified, and yet everything happened in a distant, dreamlike fashion. The images shifted, and she saw her failure as the innumerable alphas refused to give up. One after another, they subdued her and made her their own. She saw herself tied to each of them at the arm, only able to move when they moved.

Bailey knew what was happening; it was her fear of being married off, treated by her own people as a tool or prize. It was the reverse image of the joy and relief she'd felt so recently when Fenris' proclamation had freed her from that hated tradition. Escaping what she saw before her was one of the main reasons she'd been so eager to chase shamanhood.

The spirit spoke again. "Is this it? Do you seek to become

a shaman just to flee a duty you consider undesirable? Do you truly care about the wellbeing of packs beyond your own and Weres besides yourself? Duty to all lycanthropes is the shaman's ultimate task. Do you think you can do that if your only motive is escape from circumstances you dislike?"

She almost burst into tears—the kind of hot, angry tears a child succumbs to when they feel betrayed. When adults lead them into a rhetorical trap they have no way of understanding or preparing for. The unfairness of a situation where, because the child could not expect what was to come, they had no other option than to be wrong.

But the spirit had said that her *honesty* would be judged.

"Yes," she replied in a choked voice, "but only in part. At first, that was one of the biggest perks—the notion of being free from *having* to marry some guy just because the old rules say so. But it's not the only reason. The more I've learned, the more I realize how important it is to give something back. I never fit in very well among Weres, but since Fenris showed up, I have a way that suits me. With us all under attack, it's like I have a larger obligation to help."

The spirit, its wolf form again coalescing out of blue light as the phantoms of Bailey's fears wavered out of sight, looked at her and waited.

"I have the power and the potential to make a differ-ence. A good one. And I want to; I didn't even realize how much I wanted to. What I thought I wanted, starting out, isn't what's driving me now. I see how much more there is to it."

She wasn't sure if she'd worded it as well as she could have. Maybe she wasn't being clear or eloquent, but it was the truth.

The ghostly wolf nodded its great head. "So be it. We believe you, Bailey. And you have passed the first test."

Had she been in the woods, she might have slumped against a tree in relief.

"But," the spirit went on, "your trials are not yet concluded. There are many more in the battery to come. Some will move beyond conversations of the soul into the realm of the physical."

Well, she thought, and half-wondered if the spirit could hear her think, *that's something I have experience with.*

"Now," said the wolf, "there is another thing we must know. Can you choose between what is best for your people on the one hand and what your heart desires on the other?"

Her gut clenched and she felt like she might be falling, having sensed the implication of the entity's words.

Horror nearly overwhelmed her as a new image reared up from the blackness. Roland, standing alone, his usual calm confidence shaken and his handsome face drawn with sudden vulnerability, surrounded by angry Weres. Attacking him with intent to kill.

CHAPTER FIVE

Wolves crashed into the wizard or were flung away by his magic, the noises of battle and pain and fury filling the void of blackness. Helplessly, the girl watched.

The faces of the lycanthropes trying to rip apart her beloved changed then, even while in beast form, they became vaguely recognizable, and a selection of them shifted back into humanoids. There was no mistaking them: people from her town, individuals she had known her whole life.

"No," Bailey groaned. "Stop this. It isn't right. You make this stop right now!"

She could no longer see the wolf-spirit, but its voice echoed above the din. "Name a side in the struggle," it announced, "and reinforce your conviction with action. Do that, and it will end."

Once more, she fought to keep from crying; it was too much.

Will Waldsbach was among the attackers and he fell back screaming, his hair on fire and his arms burnt. A guy with whom Bailey had gone to high school collapsed with a deep plasma wound in his stomach. Roland was bleeding from eight or ten different wounds as the enraged Weres tore at and slashed his slim body.

Each blow struck, regardless of who was the recipient, was mirrored in the core of Bailey's being. Everyone's pain was hers too.

"*No*," she shouted, gathering the power of her magic and unleashing it all as a wave of pure arcane force. Its raw, elemental strength disrupted the vision and pushed away the manifestations, so they grew smaller and fainter and moved in slow motion.

Off to the side, she saw the spirit watching. It seemed undisturbed by her action.

She seized the opportunity amidst the brief and temporary silence to declare that she'd made a decision.

"I choose *both* sides," she said, "because the reasons behind this fight were never explained to me. *Why* are they fighting? I don't know that, so I can't know who to side with. Shamans aren't supposed to just throw magic around and kill everyone whenever something seems to go wrong, are they? And we're not just guardians, either. We're supposed to…be wise, lead, arbitrate disputes, and that sort of thing."

The spectral wolf listened patiently, and the terrible vision of the battle remained a pale and distant echo of the vividness it had had a moment ago.

"You didn't tell me what led to this clusterfuck," Bailey continued. "You just threw a bunch of random violence in front of my face. If I'm going to be a spiritual leader to my people and all that, I can't do reckless, stupid things. Even if I've been reckless in the past, which I'm aware I have, I have to step up now and do things the smart way. That includes figuring out the sources of problems and hearing the different sides of the story so I can lessen the worst of the damage or solve the conflict. Tell me I'm wrong."

The void grew quiet as the image of the battle vanished.

"You are not wrong," said the wolf. "You have proven that you possess the beginnings of the wisdom you'll require."

Then it dissolved back into a blotchy mass of light that then faded, and the blackness swirled. The girl felt like she was falling, only to sit straight up and open her eyes.

She gasped. It was over, and she was back in the temple gallery amidst the statues and blue torches. Her wolves had formed a protective circle around her unconscious body through the ordeal. They all stared in wonder.

"I'm okay," she told them as her racing pulse slowed to normal.

Will knelt beside her. "Good. We were worried, but we figured you could do it. You've been out for...I dunno, at least an hour. I can't tell time in this place. And that ghost-wolf thing vanished at the same time you passed out. What happened?"

She was about to explain to the best of her ability when the echoing phantasmal voice rang through the hall.

"We were inside her," it stated. "Within her mind and heart. She has been found worthy thus far."

Faces broke into grins or relaxed with the dismissal of

tension. A few big hands patted the young woman on the back.

"But," the spirit added, "the internal test is but the first. Next comes the test of flesh and bone, muscle, and sinew—and we shall see if your worth is equal in that realm. Proceed!"

Without further explanation, the widely dispersed sapphire glow reconstituted in lupine form and led them under a stone arch into a narrow passage that led to someplace deeper in the temple. It was lit only by residual light from the large chamber, and there was barely room for them to walk single file. Bailey was behind the apparition, and her Weres came after her in tight formation.

When the passage was almost totally black, a new source of light as blue as the specter appeared ahead. After moving toward it, they emerged into a room the same size as the previous one and showing a similar aesthetic, although the details were noticeably different.

Low, broad-rimmed stone bowls lined the sides of the floor, and blue flames burned within each container. The fuel looked like piles of silvery-black crystals. Here there were no pillars dividing the room into informal sectors. Instead, there were broad pedestals topped with more statues.

Bailey peered at them as she wandered in. If the previous chamber had been devoted to humanoid shamans and normal wolves, this one belonged to lycanthropes in their powerful animalistic forms. Many of the sculptures looked familiar.

"Holy shit," Will gasped. "Are these…"

Everyone knew the answer. They gazed upon representations of the great and influential alphas of the past, fighters, leaders, and heroes. Legendary figures, all.

Roger gestured to an especially massive wolf statue. "Look. It's Lonchagne du Astrom, the guy who fought off about a hundred pissed-off raiders who were trying to mob his settlement. That was in Brittany, I think, back in the goddamn Dark Ages. Eighth Century or thereabouts."

It was true, Bailey realized. Her history was fuzzy, but now that the young man had pointed it out, she did recognize the figure. And she was impressed with Roger's knowledge. He was smarter than he'd seemed at first.

The rest of the Weres fanned out around the chamber, examining the other statues and naming the ones they knew, whose deeds were every bit as illustrious as Lonchagne's. Their awe and excitement were palpable; this was a museum to the heroism of the lycanthrope species.

Bailey realized she couldn't see the guiding spirit anymore, but its voice reverberated over the stones at that moment.

"You revere them as good Weres should," it intoned. "But how would you fare against them in combat?"

Oh, shit! Bailey almost slapped herself in the face.

Out loud, she shouted, "Gather over here! By me!" hardly a second too soon.

The statue of Lonchagne was cracking apart. Or rather, its surface was cracking like the shell of an egg, revealing shining fur and rippling sheets of muscle beneath. The stone pieces struck the floor, sending vibrations through it. Then a low growl sounded in the dank subterranean air.

The eleven young Weres formed a cluster near the chamber's entrance just in time to see the legendary beast's head turn to them. The eyes burned with a bestial but righteous fury, primitive and unwavering. Then it pounced.

A huge streak like tarnished silver was all they saw at first, then half of them reeled away, spilling out around the pedestals and narrowly avoiding the braziers of blue flame. The others, realizing battle was unavoidable, shifted into wolf form.

Bailey spun toward Lonchagne, who was half again more massive than the largest Were she could recall ever seeing. He was probably larger than her bestial form. One of Roger's boys was backed against the wall, and the legendary wolf's jaws were open and ready to strike.

The werewitch threw everything she had at the monster. A horizontal tornado of wind, fire, and electrified water spiraled out from her hands and smashed into the giant wolf's haunches, kicking up so much visual interference that she couldn't tell what effect it might have had. Out of the corners of her eyes, she saw her companions leaping around on four legs in a mad frenzy of fear and belligerence.

The smoke cleared. Roger's friend had finally jumped clear and shifted, and Lonchagne was unharmed. All Bailey had done was to draw the beast's attention toward herself.

"Crap," she breathed.

Suddenly Lonchagne was airborne and Bailey hurled herself aside, rolling under and then behind one of the fire bowls. The air whistled as the fangs of the wolf passed behind her head, and his tremendous mass bowled her toward the wall. He crashed into it with enough force to make the ground shudder.

Three of the Weres pounced on Lonchagne, biting and clawing at his face, only to be shouldered or swatted aside with ease and tumble against the stones. Seeing this, Bailey realized their foe could have killed them yet hadn't.

On the other hand, they couldn't beat him with their current tactics. Especially not when her magic seemed to have no effect.

Another statue was cracking too. Fighting two creatures of Lonchagne's power would be impossible.

She lunged forward, aiming to fight fire with proverbial fire. Her bones and tendons and muscles elongated, black hair sprouted through her skin, and her skull reconfigured itself. By the time her forelegs hit the ground, she'd grown big enough to challenge even Lonchagne. Her eyes went red, filtering her vision through a crimson screen.

Her jaws lashed out as she bounded forward and seized their enemy by his left rear ankle, holding him back from his next charge and almost tripping him. In a second or two, he'd turn on her and crush her, but it was enough time for Roger to leap at Lonchagne's head, locking his claws around the huge wolf's neck and pulling him off-balance.

Bailey sent her mind out, using what magic she could to communicate with her followers via telepathy.

Rally by me, she called, using psychic vibrations rather than sound. *We need to fight as a unit. Take out the legs while the rest pile all over him.*

Three Weres seized Lonchagne's other limbs, and another five slammed into his head, neck, and torso. Behind them, the second statue had just finished coming to life, and a third was cracking as well.

Lonchagne roared and snarled, heaving his massive

body from side to side, but he dislodged only two of his attackers. The rest bore him to the ground, overwhelming him with their numbers and coordinated ferocity. Suddenly the monster was still, as though stone once again.

Then the second of the legendary wolves slammed into their midst, with the third close behind.

Again! Bailey cried. *Anyone left over after we immobilize that one, go after the next one and protect the first group! Harry and harass but don't engage until the rest are freed up.*

Somehow, it worked, though at least three of her companions suffered injuries. But they had a frenzy of momentum behind them, and they'd found an effective strategy.

One by one, the ancient heroes went down, each one more quickly than the last, even as the statues came to life with increasing frequency. Mere minutes later, it seemed, Bailey's pack stood victorious over a dozen large, immobile wolf shapes.

The werewitch shifted back into her human form, and most of those who followed her did likewise. Roger, who'd fought with a level of abandon that went straight past bravery into craziness, was badly bruised and slashed. He probably had broken ribs, and he had lost enough blood to be getting lightheaded. Bailey helped two others bind his wounds with his ripped-up shirt.

"Well, Roger," Bailey told him, "you sure as shit proved you're willing to get your ass kicked on my behalf, and we wouldn't have won without you. Stay near the back until we get through this. You've done your part for today."

"I'll do as you say," he gasped, "but I can still fight."

She narrowly avoided laughing, although it would have

been a nervous chuckle since he was at serious risk in his current state. "In that case, you can be the last man standing if it comes to that. But you're off the front lines until further notice. You'll thank me later."

The flickering azure radiance around them thickened near the center of the chamber, and again the wolf spirit addressed them.

"Congratulations," it said. "You have demonstrated a key fact—the greatest strength of both shaman and alpha is in the strength they give to the pack. Unity of Weres against outside threats, cooperation and coordination, is mighty enough to overcome legends. The greatest and most powerful of past alphas can go only so far without the other Weres behind and beside them."

Bailey nodded, knowing she couldn't claim this victory as hers alone.

"And," the spirit extrapolated, "you, Bailey, might be a werewitch, but magic is not the only way to solve problems. It is rare, and you can fill that niche when you must, but you cannot eschew the part of you that is a shifter just like the rest of your people. Use that ability too, and rely on the strength of the group. Now, rest, recover from your wounds, and think about what I have said."

Relieved, they all slumped against the walls, restful peace replacing the tension of battle.

The wolf spirit remained silent and placid near the center as time passed. It felt like hours, and soon the pack had the sensation of having woken up from a long night's sleep. Even Roger seemed slightly better.

Bailey blinked, wondering if some obscure spell had

further distorted the Other's already warped temporal regimen.

She intoned, "Is everyone okay for the next trial?"

"Hell, yeah," Will told her. "I feel better than I did when we started."

Others laughed and agreed. Roger again asked to be out front, but Bailey had to gently refuse. For all that he'd supernaturally improved, he was still the most beaten-up of the eleven of them.

The phantasmal guide moved closer to the group, but it made no further announcements.

"Okay," Bailey said, "we're ready. What's next?"

To her consternation, the spirit didn't answer her question, but only drifted a little nearer, its lupine face forming out of the shifting mass of light as it examined her.

"Now," it began, in a softer voice than it had used thus far, "we wish to know more about you, Bailey Nordin. We've tested the raw mettle of your body and your soul and your wiliness to fight together with our kind. But we are curious about other things."

She shifted her stance, mildly uncomfortable with the notion that she might have to talk about deeply personal matters in front of everyone. The spirit hadn't, after all, taken her to an inner mental plane as it had during the first trial. This was happening right here, with ten young men standing around listening.

What if it asks about Roland? If it does, well, then I guess it's time for everyone to learn. I meant to tell them anyway.

"Bailey," asked the ghost, "what is the story of your life? Who are you? Tell us. We wish to know about your upbringing. The fears and insecurities you've always struggled with, beyond your desire to avoid marriage. Your feelings about your place among your people, and your relationships with humans. The greatest challenges you face these days in your corner of Earth in whatever year it currently is. *Everything.*"

She closed her eyes a few seconds, took a deep breath, and forged ahead.

For starters, she gave the spirit a brief summary of her early existence. Basic stuff, like how she was born into the Nordin family, who'd lived in the Hearth Valley of Oregon for at least five generations, having come to America from somewhere in Sweden over a century ago. She knew practically nothing about her ancestors' history in the old country, except that lycanthropy went back as far as anyone could remember.

She related a bit about her school days and what she was like as a kid—a tomboy who mostly played with males, Weres, and humans alike, at least until puberty. Then the dynamics had shifted, and the Weres all wondered when she'd grow out of it. The rejection she'd suffered for her being unable to shift, which, by the standards of her people, was a disability.

That drove her to associate more with humans. Aside from her brothers, of course.

She gave the short version of how, ever since she'd graduated, life had seemed like an ongoing exercise in pretending the doom of a forced mating wasn't hanging over her head. Half the time, she was angry and looking for excuses to get into fights, hoping it might prove something and convince people to leave her alone.

Then she'd finally met Roland and discovered her latent

powers. In the space of a couple months, everything had changed.

The blue light around the spirit gently pulsed like a heartbeat as it listened.

"Roland is important to you?" it asked.

Bailey had expected a question like that, so she didn't blush or flinch. "Yeah," she admitted. "We've gotten pretty close. He's been by my side through all of this, but even if he wasn't around, I'd want to keep stepping up and doing things *right*. To the best of my ability."

Then she offered a shrug. "As always with stuff like this, though, it's easier said than done."

The moon-like eyes of the wolf closed for a moment before reopening. "That is commendable, Bailey. You were not originally chosen for this path. No one led you down the road to shamanhood until very recently. Under normal circumstances, you would have begun your training at a far younger age. Many packs select their prospective shamans as children to begin quietly molding them well ahead of the point when they must undergo the trials."

She tilted her head vaguely. *That's about what I expected. Something that ought to have a whole upbringing behind it, rather than something you rush through at the last minute like I've been doing. Then again, haven't I always been behind everyone else?*

The spirit went on, "Selecting potential shamans as children helps ensure they will turn out properly in terms of their personality and mindset and gives them the advantage of preparing for what's to come as young adults. Of course, no method is perfect. No amount of training can suffice if the child does not have the requisite magical aptitude. Werewitches have the greatest gifts of all. You have taken this as it's come, remaining brave and earnest, and that will count in your favor."

"Well, thank you," Bailey quipped, nudging her toe against the floor.

The wolf turned around. "The next trial awaits. Come this way."

The werewitch and her pack followed the specter around the flaming bowls and through tumbled wreckage of the chamber, coming at length to the opening of another narrow tunnel. The way it was carved, combined with the lay of shadows versus light in the chamber, had hidden it from sight earlier.

"Proceed," said the spirit, standing aside as Bailey led the way in. The other ten lycanthropes filed behind, with Roger near the back. Another young man in better condition brought up the rear.

The hallway was not long, and the girl emerged at the other end after what felt like half a minute or less of walking. Once inside the next chamber, she walked a few paces on ahead to give her Weres room. Then she stopped.

The ceiling here was so high she couldn't see it, lost in the deepening gloom. In fact, there was no obvious lighting, only a faint luminescence that seemed to emanate from the high, flat, smooth stone walls, which rose tight to either side. They had passed through a short, narrow hall into what looked like a higher, wider one. It extended straight ahead but might have bent around some distance onward. It was hard to tell.

As the last of the Weres wandered into the new passage,

the grinding of stone came from behind them, followed by a loud crash that shook the ground. Bailey spun.

A slab had fallen in the narrow corridor. They were trapped here, with no way to go but forward.

Madame Villalobos would have preferred to have a coven of at least thirteen witches with her, but seven would have to suffice. The Order's personnel were already badly taxed by the burgeoning conflict. In this case, given the importance of the targets, they had subscribed to a philosophy of quality over quantity. That gave her greater confidence in their success.

"It is beautiful here," she told the six women under her, "but do not allow yourselves to be distracted. We are close to our destination."

The nocturnal paradise of the lycanthropes' sacred realm, hidden in a far corner of the Other, was a place none of them had seen; in fact, it had been hidden from other species for many generations. They all gawked at the silvered wilderness as they walked.

But none of the others challenged Villalobos' proclamations. They were professionals—veteran operatives, every one of them. Perrault and Blasko had accompanied her during their attempted truce with Roland for that very reason.

And the other four, though younger and less powerful, were considered promising initiates with several combat-oriented missions under their belts.

"Madame," asked one of the newer girls, "is it possible

that the wizard is somewhere far from the werewitch? The briefings said that the two of them have, in the past, separated for long stretches while training."

Villalobos frowned as she felt a ripple of uncertainty flow through the rudimentary coven-mind they had established. It was a good question, she supposed; it indicated that the younger agent was applying her critical thinking skills. But it irked her and undermined the team's confidence in their course of action.

"Yes, it is possible," she replied, "but not likely. Why would he be here in the werewolves' holy land unless he was aiding or escorting Bailey?"

The other witch nodded, and the group's *esprit de corps* regained most of its strength.

Although the moonlit forest was treacherous and labyrinthine in its way, the subtle beacon did not fail them. Madame Villalobos had noticed its signal growing stronger in the few minutes since she'd last spoken.

When she, Perrault, and Blasko had confronted Roland to try to negotiate his defection away from the Weres, they had placed an incredibly subtle and devious tracking spell on him. The magic behind it was new and sufficiently complex and mysterious that even Villalobos did not understand it fully. Madame Dorleac, the second in command of the Order, had taught it to her before they'd departed for the United States.

It was virtually untraceable. They had no reason to believe that the foolish, handsome, and apparently smitten wizard suspected they'd been following him.

They trekked up higher and rockier ground, where

lupine symbols appeared on stones and trees, and sensed they were nearing a plateau.

Villalobos raised her hand in a signal to stop. Everyone froze in place.

Creeping forward and masking her presence with magic, the witch peered through a veil of leaves and saw a great stone temple like an ancient step pyramid rising from the green moor of the clearing beyond. Standing before a wall of mist that surrounded the structure were two figures.

She recognized both. Roland's lanky frame and golden hair marked him first, but the other could hardly be mistaken, either—a tall, broad-shouldered man in a bulky, hooded coat. They'd seen him in the vision when he'd intervened and killed the three American volunteers over a week ago.

And they knew who he was. He could no longer hide his identity.

Villalobos returned to her squad. "Roland is there, and the so-called Marcus. They are waiting outside the lycanthropes' temple. We will strike directly. The wizard is to be overwhelmed and taken alive if possible. The other…let me deal with him. He dares not intervene—not this time."

"And then?" asked Perrault.

"Then," the leader continued, "we force our way into the building. Bailey is certainly in there."

The younger witch who'd questioned her before spoke up. "Madame, if the temple is consecrated to werewolves, would it have magical defenses against intruders who are not of their kind?"

Villalobos frowned. The troublemaker's name was

Holopainen, she recalled, a Finnish girl who was accounted something of a prodigy. She had a penetrating mind, but she would need to learn to keep her mouth shut when her superiors had decided on a course of action.

"If they do," Villalobos stated, "we will break them asunder."

CHAPTER SIX

The first passage ended at a crossroads, but "cross" wasn't the right shape to describe it since the path branched off in five directions rather than four.

"Fuckin' shit," Bailey growled. "It's a maze. I hate those goddamn things."

Instantly she wished she hadn't said that. Degenerating into a fit of cursing might make it look like she was losing control and erode her pack's faith in her leadership. However, what was done was done.

Will stepped up beside her. "Okay, so should we split up? That way, if one group hits a dead end, they can shout to the other group and we meet back up at a point farther along."

Bailey considered it, but only briefly. "No, I don't think so. I see your reasoning, but we don't know what the hell's out there. Some passages might lead so far from the rest of the maze that we couldn't hear each other's shouts. Or there might be…enemies in there. Not a fun thing to think about, but we have to consider it."

Grimacing, the South Cliff alpha gave a nod and folded his arms over his chest. "Yeah, I think you're right. We need to stick together, but it'll take longer."

"It will," Bailey conceded, "but we're not in a hurry, although I'd like to be done with this as much as the rest of you. Time passes slower in here, and we don't have to deal with thirst or sleep or anything. For now, we work as a pack. Everyone stays together no matter where we end up or what jumps out at us or anything."

The Weres grunted their assent. One raised a hand, though.

"Which way do we start? There are four passages besides the one we came down. Do you think there's any way to know the right answer?"

Bailey looked around, but no one had any bright ideas.

"If," she began, "there was a clue as to the right path earlier in the temple, I guess we missed it. So let's just pick one, and then it'll be a process of elimination."

Another guy chimed in, "In old-school gaming, like, dungeon-crawl tabletop shit, the tradition was that you always started off going right. Right, right, right every time, then you started to work your way back through the lefts."

"Okay, so be it." The werewitch shrugged.

They started with the corridor that branched off farthest to the right. Bailey and Will were in the lead, with the rest of the wolves coming two and three abreast several paces back.

To everyone's relief, the way was simple and linear. At first. After five minutes of walking, it bent around at a right angle and then they came to another split, although in this case, there were only two options—right and left.

"Okay, halt for a sec," said Bailey. "Decision time once more. Let's look around."

She was hoping to find an indicator that felt right. Some vague indication that one path was better than another, but so far, they both looked the same, stretching between identical stone walls leading into identical cocoons of darkness.

Then she thought she saw a shape moving in the corner of her vision. It scuttled around the corner between the left-hand hallway and the way they'd just come. Her head snapped toward it.

There was nothing there.

"Did anybody else see that?" she asked. "Looked like something moved by fast."

A couple of the Weres answered. "Yeah, I did."

"Me too."

Two others thought they had, but weren't sure. The rest seemed confused, having seen nothing.

All of them were suddenly on edge, given the dreary nature of the labyrinth, the exertion of the trials they'd already faced, and the prospect that they could be lost in here for hours upon hours with hostile beings attacking them from the shadows. The combination of factors was pushing them to the limits of their self-control.

And again, a dark shape flitted by, now in the far right of Bailey's peripheral vision.

"Shit!" she snapped. "The hell's going on? Here, I'm gonna conjure up some light."

Raising her hands, she generated a white ball of illumination about five feet above and in front of her, bathing the area around them in its bright glow. Somehow, the shadows farther down the halls were too deep and thick to be dispelled.

A Were along the side snarled, "*There!* That's the fucker!"

Before Bailey could react, the man who'd spoken had shifted and was bounding on all fours down the left-hand corridor.

"Get back here!" Bailey barked. "Stop it! We need you here, goddammit!"

Two other Weres were moving in that direction as well. "We'll bring him back!" one of them cried out. Then they changed, and another pair of wolves vanished into the black unknown in pursuit of the first.

Bailey half-jumped after them, then stopped firmly, turning to stare at the rest of the pack.

"No one else runs off!" she commanded. "We gotta stick together. I mean it. Next guy who tries to go off on his own, I'll singe the hairs on his ass if I have to and magically glue him to the ceiling by his toes while he chills the fuck out."

"Okay," Will murmured uncertainly. "So, what do we do?"

Bailey pursed her lips. "We go after them. But we move as a group, nobody splitting away from the rest until they're all safely back with us, not without my order."

She led the way, moving at a fast jog down the left hall. Will and the others crowded around her elbows or behind her, everyone's eyes scanning the corridor both ahead and to the sides as they moved.

The path bent around a corner once again, and as they rounded it, they saw another four-way crossroads before them.

"Crap," Bailey muttered.

Bailey stopped at the intersection so they could look down all three of the new hallways at once, but they saw no sign of their comrades. Not anything shaped like man or wolf, nor any trail or other indications of their passage. The corridors all ended in ebon gloom.

Then came a noise like a ragged, half-growling moan. It echoed down the halls in a way that made it tough to discern where it had originated. The group shifted in discomfort.

The guy who'd suggested they always take right turns spoke up. "Well, it's always bad luck to split the party during a dungeon crawl. Especially when the PCs are all lost and with a high-level monster lurking in the dark."

Judging by his flippant tone, he was probably trying to cheer them up. The problem was that his words in this context were true, and each of them knew it.

Bailey put her hands on her hips. "We're trying to un-split it. I think that sound came from the right. Hard to say, but that's my best guess unless anyone here is confident it came from someplace else."

One of the Silver Stars shrugged. "Either right or straight ahead. I don't think it came from the left."

"Right it is," declared Bailey. "Let's hope those guys who ran off heard it too and are bearing in the same direction."

They moved out at a trot, keeping the same formation they'd used a minute ago. They were hoping to run into their brethren but ready for anything. The right-hand corridor twisted its way through a series of ninety-degree angles, many of which seemed to double back in the same direction, so they rapidly became disoriented.

A T-intersection appeared ahead, and Bailey called a brief halt. Before she could examine their two options, however, the rough, moaning bellow sounded again. This time it clearly came from the right.

"That way," the werewitch indicated. "I hope it isn't one of our guys in pain. Let's move."

Will Waldsbach frowned. "Doesn't sound like a wolf."

The next hall stretched onward without bends for a hundred yards, maybe more, then it bent to the left. The pack rounded the corner, braced for whatever they might encounter.

"Whoa!" Bailey exclaimed.

Just beyond the turn stood a huge bear, larger than any she'd seen or heard of. Her brain screamed grizzly, but she knew that was incorrect. Its fur was dark brown verging on black rather than the medium brown of that species and standing on its hind legs, it was both more manlike and more muscular than a true bear should have been.

Not to mention, it was at least twelve feet tall and appeared to weigh about a thousand pounds. It opened its fanged mouth and let out another ragged, bellowing groan, then extended its dagger-tipped paws and took a step toward them.

"*Get it!*" someone shouted. Chaos erupted as the battle was joined.

One of Will's friends, already shifted into beast form, pounced on the lumbering creature, snarling and foaming at the mouth. The bear met him halfway with a sweeping haymaker, the back of its paw striking the Were on the shoulder and batting him aside with shocking ease and impunity.

Then the next four, including Will, were upon their adversary, tearing at the great furry legs and belly to little effect.

In the seconds it took for the fight to get underway, Bailey realized that her wolves were outmatched by the bear's sheer size and strength. They'd have to try a different tack to overcome it.

"Get back!" she shouted at them. "Stand aside so I can blast the fucker!"

Most of them didn't hear her, but one out front did and backed away, still growling at the monster and trying to hold its gaze as a distraction.

Bailey threw out her arms and tossed a bolt of magic at the bear's upper body. It was thrashing around too much to aim at a single point, but she'd directed it such that it ought to hit the chest, head, or neck. The bolt was composed of equal parts electricity, frigid gas, and concussive force.

It struck the beast's shoulder but seemed to glance off it. The bear was briefly stunned and growled in pain but continued fighting as though little had happened.

"God*dammit!*" Bailey exclaimed.

The werewolves were trying to use hit-and-run tactics against their larger foe, snapping at it, then darting away while another wolf attacked from behind. They did almost no damage, but they drove the bear into greater heights of frenzied anger. It roared at them loud enough to make the stones tremble.

A big guy, one of Roger's underlings, had shifted back

into human form and was trying to grapple the bear from behind. At first, Bailey was stunned by the apparent stupidity of the move, but it made sense. Weres had tremendous strength even in human form, and the bear was mostly fighting on its hind legs, so it might give them the edge.

Letting out a guttural cry, the man wrapped his muscular arms around the monster's midsection and heaved it sideways. It did not fly into the wall or fall over as they'd hoped, but it stumbled, allowing another Were in wolf form to bite its rear knee.

Then the bear shook its massive body and flung the grappler off. The man briefly flew, then smacked into the wall, where he sat dazed for a moment before climbing back to his feet.

By now, two other Weres had returned to humanoid shape and had similarly ducked in under the bear's claws to wrestle its lower body, while those still in lupine form leapt up to snap at its face. They were slowly wearing the hulking creature down, but not nearly fast enough. It would overcome them before long.

And Bailey could not get a shot in without hitting her pack.

Unexpectedly, the bear also shifted. It shrank to the proportions of a man, naked and bestial-looking. He was as much a giant by human standards as his alternate form was a colossus among bears—over seven feet tall and covered in bulging, rippling muscles.

The shock of what had just transpired gave a couple of the wolves pause, and the man plowed into them, shouldering one Were aside and knocking another unconscious with a hammer-like blow of his fist. He clinched with a third, whom he began to overpower the instant they matched strength.

Bailey feared that if she ordered the Weres to disperse, any magic attack she could throw would have little effect. Then the bear-man would maim or kill them in retaliation. Given the lack of damage caused by her first strike, the creature appeared to have at least some resistance to sorcery. She also felt as though her spellcasting abilities were dampened by the labyrinth.

She figured the only course of action was to overwhelm their enemy through force of numbers and strategic fighting.

Plowing into the fray, she drop-kicked the man in the chest, shouting, "Get the wounded away!" as she launched. Her feet crashed against the massive pectorals of the bestial man and drove him back three steps but failed to drop him.

It was enough time, though, for the Weres still standing to move the injured or unconscious away from their opponent. Bailey saw Roger pulling the guy who'd been knocked out to safety against the far wall.

She landed on her feet as two other Weres, still on all fours, distracted the bear-man by lunging at his back and side. Bailey moved in and kicked him in the groin, but he was in such a berserk frenzy that it only made him angrier. His gargantuan arm lashed out and she practically fell over, dodging it.

One hit and she'd be out. She had never fought anyone of such size and physical strength.

It occurred to her that she might be able to control her size when shifting. Normally she became a singularly large creature, which had given her problems with shredded clothes. In addition to that inconvenience, a smaller form might fare better in the tight confines of the labyrinth.

Inhaling deeply, Bailey dropped to her hands and knees and exerted her full force of will over the process of transformation. She pictured herself applying the brakes to a truck while driving downhill in the mountains, forcing it to go the minimum speed she wanted rather than careening down according to the pull of gravity.

She felt her body changing and reconfiguring and fur sprouting from her skin, but somehow she stayed within what remained of her clothes, and the relative dimensions of the hallway did not seem smaller. With a brief rush of exaltation, she grasped that she'd succeeded, having shifted into a wolf no larger than her human shape.

Feeling faster and more acrobatic than she ever had, the werewitch sprang into the fight again. While the ursine hulk turned to fight off the others, her teeth sank into the back of his leg to hamstring him. His body was so powerful that she failed to disable him, but the wound slowed him down.

As the other Weres circled, Bailey, still in wolf form, spat a continuous torrent of magic, tossing anything she could think of at the bear-man. It struck him full-on and drove him, grunting and hollering, against the wall. The stone behind him cracked.

Alphas! she called via telepathy rather than speech. *Stand guard over the wounded!*

Another burst of magic pressed their huge foe into the stone. It didn't do much damage, but it kept him pinned down. She increased the volume and intensity of the spells, still finding her abilities oddly limited, but it was enough to put the bear-man on the defensive.

Magic alone wouldn't do the trick, she knew. *Will! Attack him!* Being a good shaman meant knowing when to ask for help, and she needed it.

Will left Roger's second-in-command to guard the fallen and flung himself at the titan. Bailey kept her streams of crackling sorcery focused on the man's upper body while the South Cliff alpha snapped at his legs.

The big Silver Star Were, the one who'd tried wrestling with the bear previously, was back in the fray. He again piled into the man during an instant when Bailey let up on blasting him with magic, seizing a better hold of him now that the two were of comparable size. He dashed the were-bear's head into the stone.

Then their enemy shifted back into his beast form, the sudden explosion in his size driving the big guy back. Bailey launched a fireball at his eyes to distract him, then pounced and snapped her teeth at his throat.

As he dodged, the burly Silver Star jumped on him and astonishingly, lifted the massive beast in the air to slam him into the ground. Bailey paused for a split second in awe, then pressed her advantage and leapt toward the bear, shifting back into human form in midair and landing on him with a powerful elbow-drop. The bony protrusion of her arm crunched into the huge man's stomach, and his eyes rolled back in his head.

The wrestler type pounded the man's head with his fists while Bailey twisted his leg, grinning fiercely with the knowledge that victory was nearly theirs.

"Wish I had a ladder or a steel chair to whack this guy with," she growled.

Her companion loosed one more punch into the giant's face, and finally their adversary slumped, unconscious and drooling blood on the floor.

"Well," she panted, standing up and wiping her palms against each other, "that's not how I expected a dance with a bear in a dark room to go in 2020."

She looked up, but nobody seemed to have understood the joke. Or they were distracted by their lingering fear, growing tiredness, and the after-effects of adrenaline. She gave a sour grimace and turned back to business.

Two men were on the ground, though still alive—one of Will's, and one of Roger's. They were both banged up, possibly with minor fractures and bleeding from half a dozen small wounds. She and the others who were still on their feet helped them up and checked them over. Though compromised, they seemed able to continue.

Roger was about the same. He'd wisely hung back from the main fight and stuck to supporting activities. In his current state, if he'd tried to take the bear on, he might well have died.

"Right," the werewitch announced. "We basically have two choices. Either we can look for a way out, or we can keep looking for the rest of the pack."

No one weighed in right away, so she added, "Which, as far as I'm concerned, is only one choice. We have to find the others. Then we'll find our way out of this wretched place."

Nodding grimly and straightening up, the Weres readied themselves for further exertion and stress.

Unexpectedly, blue light coalesced behind them, and again the guardian wolf spirit addressed the group.

"Congratulations," it began, "on navigating this far into the labyrinth and defeating the great bear. You showed excellent courage and coordination. Not everyone is capable of overcoming such a mighty creature."

Her curiosity racing ahead of her thoughts, Bailey asked, "What was it? One of us? I've never seen a werebear, although it makes sense that there'd be bears along with us werewolves."

"Ursine shifters exist, just as surely as lupine ones do," the spirit explained. "But their numbers are far smaller, their members existing in isolation even from us, their distant brethren, so their presence is not so acutely felt."

Bailey marveled at that silently. She wondered if anyone she'd met back home in the northwestern mountains was secretly a werebear. If so, it wouldn't be any stranger than half the other crap she'd encountered in the last two months.

But she had other priorities. "Thanks. But now that we succeeded, is there any chance you can help me find the rest of my pack?"

The phantom's blue light dimmed. "I cannot. You must do that on your own."

She sighed. "Yeah, figures."

CHAPTER SEVEN

By this point, Roland was getting a better grip on how time passed within the Other. He and Bailey had figured out that time was not frozen within it. That it moved forward, rather than backward, so they would always emerge at a point later in their world than when they'd left. The rate was still difficult to determine, however.

He was still waiting outside the lycanthropic temple. It was impossible to say how long Bailey and her Weres had been in there, but it seemed like far too long.

"Fenris," he asked, "is there anything like a ballpark estimate of how long those trials are supposed to take? Wait, don't tell me—the answer is something like 'How long is a piece of string?' or 'What is the sound of one hand clapping?' or that sort of thing, am I right?"

The god had been standing in front of the mist barrier and aligned with the entrance, grimly staring into the depths as he waited. He slowly turned his head and looked down at Roland.

"Yes," he said.

The wizard nodded and gave a thumbs-up. "Great. Okay, just so we're clear on that. Thanks."

"If you're restless," the shaman went on, "I can transport you back to an area of the Other you're familiar with, train or spar with the local spirits. We should not fight here since it might rouse the anger of—"

"*Us,*" a female voice snapped. Both men spun toward the sound, tensing at the sight of seven leather-clad women bursting into the clearing.

Fenris thrust forth his chin. "This is holy ground, consecrated to lycanthropes only. You are trespassing and need to turn back *now,* or you will incur the wrath of the accumulated ancient spirits of our people. The great shamans and pack leaders of old are not to be trifled with."

Roland's eyes fell upon the woman in the lead with recognition that quickly turned to malice. "Villalobos, was it? So much for your peace mission—unless you've come to offer your unconditional surrender, which would be a damn good idea on your part. So you know, all you have to do is—"

His answer was a storm of magic, seven bursts flying at him from different directions. Not powerful enough to break through the shield he immediately raised, but more than enough to busy him with self-defense.

The barrier he created—still glowing greenish, since he hadn't had time to concentrate on a nice transparent one—crackled as he waved his arms, already straining to keep the blasts from penetrating and killing him.

"*What,*" he bellowed, "are you doing? How crazy *are* you people?"

Villalobos smiled. "We are not trying to kill you, Roland. Only to stop you from getting hurt."

"Well, this isn't the best way of showing it!" he threw back. For good measure, he also threw back three of the magical bursts, which arced like purple and green comets back toward their casters.

The witches to the sides ducked, and Villalobos caught and neutralized the projectile headed for her face. It fizzled out in a puff of steam.

Fenris had done nothing. To Roland's disbelief and anger, all he did was stand there watching with a solemn, smoldering glare.

"Roland," the lead sorceress said again, "stop this nonsense and come with us. We are only trying to rescue you from the dangerous wolves who have corrupted your mind, perverted your desires, and are using you for your power. Squandering it. You have far too much potential to waste it in their service like a pet. Come with us instead. Besides, we don't wish people to think we have any ill will toward other witches."

Roland's jaw dropped. "Ill will? Here, let me show you some fucking *ill will*."

At a vicious swipe of his hand, the concentrated energies of the remaining attacks they'd flung at him, combined with three times more of his own, rocketed toward their position like the initial explosion of an erupting volcano. The storm of elemental, arcane, telekinetic, and psionic force struck them with such speed and force that for a brief instant, it seemed that he'd blotted them out.

But the witches were too strong to be overcome so quickly. They'd had to divert all their energies into defending themselves, with each of the seven doing her part to absorb, redirect, or neutralize the furious mass of deadly magic. Far too soon for Roland's liking, four of them had things under control again, while the three most powerful ones counterattacked.

He reeled before the assault. Deadly waves of lightning, fire, ice, wind, and acid rained down on him. The earth buckled under his feet, and his mind reeled from psionic spells designed to drive him to terror or despair or befuddlement. Storms of blades made of pure arcane essence threatened to skewer and incinerate him. He was a wizard of unusually strong talents, but the Venatori had sent their best this time, and he was hopelessly outnumbered.

"Fenris!" the wizard shouted. "Why the hell aren't you helping me, goddammit?"

"Because he is not allowed to!" Villalobos laughed, sadistic triumph in her voice. "We know who he is. The ruse is ended!"

Gritting his teeth, Roland managed to repulse most of the magical blasts coming his way, but the witches easily dodged or blocked them and continued their onslaught. There was no way he could counterattack effectively at this point. For all his talents, he had to devote one hundred percent of his magical powers to keeping himself from being reduced to a melted patch on the grass.

"Bullshit!" He scoffed. "Marcus—Fenris! You helped us before, didn't you?"

He recalled the shaman intervening two weeks ago when he and Bailey had been attacked in the Other by a trio of the Venatori's American patsies. Fenris had swept in and utterly destroyed the sorceresses. They had been weak enough that the wizard and werewitch could have done it themselves, but still. Now, in the current struggle against seven witches who were far more powerful, he was refusing to enter the fight.

Roland abruptly remembered he had mentioned something about how his intervention could cause severe consequences.

"It's true," Fenris stated, his voice edged with anger but restrained.

"You see?" Perrault, the Frenchwoman agreed. "There is nothing you can do, Roland. Now is the time for you to surrender and come with us."

The wizard almost collapsed from despair. When he needed help the most was the one time he couldn't get it. Although his abilities were sufficient to keep the Venatori from killing him, he couldn't hold out indefinitely, not against all seven. If he struggled on, after a while, he'd pass out from exhaustion, and they'd take him prisoner anyway.

"Fenris!" he called again. "What do you think they plan to do? They're going in after Bailey once they've captured me! For fuck's sake!"

"If he aids you," Villalobos jeered, "he risks the entire world. An attack by a deity upon the people of another deity will bring about a conflict between gods. All living things on the planet would be caught up in it. Even werewolves are not so stupid as to risk *that!*"

Fenris shook his head. "I cannot act directly against them, not with my identity known. Even with my own people, the Weres, my powers and privileges are limited by ancient pacts that I can't just go around breaking. I can guide and teach, I can demonstrate, I can keep troublesome alphas or lone wolves in line with careful shows of force, but that is all. A battle between Freya and me would cause untold devastation, and since I'd be the one who broke the pact, other gods would side with her, and we would not have much hope of winning."

Squeezing back tears, Roland thought of Bailey. If she burst out of the temple right now, the two of them might be able to win this. If she didn't, all he could do was wish her luck.

Close to total exhaustion, he allowed his shield to weaken. Madame Villalobos fired a lance of concussive force and psionic confusion straight through it, striking him in the face. He flew back to crash against the barrier of solid mist, slumping in semi-consciousness.

Cackling with glee, the sorceresses advanced beyond the threshold of the woods and into the clearing to claim their prize. Two of the younger and weaker among their number seized Roland, shackling him with chains engraved with anti-magic runes and pulling him to his feet as his head lolled.

Villalobos folded her gloved hands in front of her. "Take him back for questioning and debriefing," she ordered the pair. "At once. Then one of you shall return."

The Spaniard spread a hand and opened a shimmering violet portal, and the two witches and their prisoner vanished into it. It seemed that only a minute or two had passed when one of the Venatori came back through.

"It is done," she reported. "He has been delivered to the others, who will see to him."

"Good." Madame Villalobos turned to the wall of magical fog, conjured a white-hot sword blade of arcane plasma, and used it to cut through the barrier, holding it open as her followers stepped through. They turned to smirk at Fenris.

The humanoid god glared at them with undisguised loathing. "I will warn you one more time," he thundered. "I might not be able to stop you, but there are other entities that can and *will*. This is your last chance to turn back. You're making a mistake, and you won't like the consequences."

Villalobos ignored him and stepped through. The mist sealed behind her.

"Pay no heed to that fool," she told her acolytes. "He is a god of dumb beasts. And now, let us go fetch the ones who are even lower in the food chain than he is."

With a confidence bordering on arrogance, the six witches strode through the dark entrance of the pyramid and were lost from sight.

Fenris remained behind, clenching and unclenching his powerful hands.

"Good luck, Bailey," he muttered under his breath. "You're going to need it more than ever."

"Sound off," Bailey commanded, "or stand there while I count your heads. Need to make sure we're not down any other guys besides the ones who ran off."

They obeyed, and she went over them quickly to ensure they hadn't lost anyone else. Everyone was present, save the three who'd sprinted after the mysterious shape in the dark.

After another short break to get their bearings, the group set back off into the maze in search of their lost comrades. They proceeded in the direction they'd been going before the bear had appeared, and they continued to follow the strategy of always taking right turns unless a reason popped up that indicated otherwise.

But no such justification ever appeared. They saw nothing, heard nothing, and found nothing.

Roger, struggling against the feverish delirium threatened by his injuries, asked, "Do you think they might have gotten out of the maze by now? Maybe they're back in that other hall we came from, or they're on the other side of it."

"Could be," said Bailey. "But if we get out the other side and they're not waiting for us, we'll just have to go back in looking for them. Too bad nobody has a pen and paper. We could have at least started making a map."

The guy who'd made the dungeon-crawling reference chimed in. "I already checked my cell phone, and it's not getting any service. Who woulda thunk? Half a mile underground in a parallel dimension. Shouldn't all this magical stuff function like a signal booster? What a fuckin' rip-off, man."

The werewitch gave a low chuckle, but then she thought of something. "Signals. Hey, Will? Roger? And anyone else. Do you guys, or other alphas, have a call or distinctive sound you can make that the others would recognize? Like, a universal wolf code or that kind of thing?"

Will widened his eyes in appreciation. "Yeah, honestly, I know one. I dunno if they'll be able to hear since we don't know how far away they are, or if this stupid labyrinth will block the sound, but it's worth a shot."

Bailey gestured to him. "Do it, then."

The South Cliff alpha shifted to beast form, his loose clothes tightening around his second shape as he elongated and sprouted sepia fur. Then he raised his head as if to howl at the moon, but the sound that emerged was low and understated, almost infrasonic to the humanoid ear. She *felt* it more than heard it.

Silence reigned over the maze. They heard no reply.

Bailey looked at the wolf. "Stay shifted. Keep doing that every time we turn a corner or come to an intersection, or what feels like every five minutes. There's a chance some *other* fucking thing will hear and come after us, but we've got to risk it. The pack can't stay split like this."

They continued through the trackless succession of dim corridors and blind angles, Will sending out his locating call here and there, but receiving no answer.

Fortunately, that meant that no hostile entities had heard them either, but the peace and silence of the corridors were deceptive.

She told herself as they paused to rest and check things out at a crossroads, *There's no way this will be so easy in the end. It isn't through with us yet, and I think things will get worse before they get better.*

Heading out again, they opted to move in a staggered line, with the first four consisting of Bailey, Will, one South Cliff, and one Silver Star. In the rear group were Roger, the big guy who'd helped Bailey wrestle the bear, and two others. That way, if they were attacked from a dark corner, they could not all be surrounded at once. One group, if threatened, could expect the other group to rush in and flank their adversary.

They'd traversed only two more corners when Bailey became aware that she'd made a terrible mistake.

Behind her came the dreadful and sickening sound of heavy stone grinding against stone, and a tremor went through the floor and walls. She spun around and saw the sides of the corridor shifting—two stone slabs reconfiguring their positions in the space between the two groups.

"No!" Bailey cried, flinging herself toward the revolving wall, but she was too late. It slammed in her face like a trapdoor, and the rear quartet's cries of alarm were instantly muffled.

Will and the others were by her side as she felt around the edges of the monolithic slab and kicked at its base, helplessly looking for a mechanism that might reverse the trap. She found none.

One of the Weres raised a hand. "We can probably meet back up with them around one of these corners. Can't be far. Uh, unless both these corridors funnel us in opposite directions."

"Yeah." Bailey grunted. "Everyone, stand back! I'm going to knock this wall down. You guys on the other side—if you can hear us, get clear! I'm gonna blast it."

The other three wolves scattered, and Bailey backed up to the opposite wall. Then, sucking air between her teeth, she unleashed a magical projectile against the thick mass of stone.

Lights flashed as the spell took the form of a spear made from heat, electricity, kinetic energy, and gravitational force. It struck the wall in the center and simply vanished.

Bailey stood blinking. Rather than dissipate or fizzle as magic usually did when it was useless, the arcane lance appeared to have sunk into the stone as though the wall were an insubstantial illusion. But that couldn't be the case. Bailey had just put her hands on it a moment ago, and it had been as solid as steel.

"What the hell?" someone behind her marveled.

Mentally clamping down on the frustrated rage welling up within her, Bailey tried another conjuration—a narrow cyclone of cold wind, dust, and freezing gases. It too was absorbed by the wall.

She let her breath out in a long, slow sigh. "That's not gonna work. It might actually be a good thing that this place is protected against magic users flinging their stuff around, including werewitches as well as hostile species. Now we're split into *three* groups. Goddammit."

Will laid a hand on her shoulder, his touch strong but gentle. "No way to go but forward. If all else fails, the four of us might be able to complete the trials, and then the temple will let everyone else go, maybe? I don't like it either since we're supposed to look out for our packs, but *someone* has to get through this maze."

"Yeah, I agree." Bailey turned to the remaining pair. "Onward, my friends. This place hasn't beaten us yet."

With the hallway that stretched ahead fading into near-total darkness, blacker even than the gloom they'd pushed through so far, she had to admit that it was making a hell of an effort.

CHAPTER EIGHT

Bailey stopped, and it occurred to her that her mouth was hanging open. "Well, I'll be damned."

They'd found their way out of the labyrinth, having come down the darkest hall yet to a chamber beyond, rather like the ones they'd passed through during the earlier trials.

What they had not done, though, was find the rest of the Weres. Bailey's group consisted of a grand total of four.

The room beyond the corridor was square and noticeably smaller than the two before the start of the maze, although still equal to a large living room or a good-sized lobby. It was barren of pillars or statues, containing only a stone dais, off-center toward the far end of the space. The dais was rectangular, and looked as though two things were meant to stand on it side by side.

Beyond the platform were two doorways leading to shadowed paths beyond. An engraved sign was affixed to the wall just above each door. The inscriptions were in a strange runic language, yet her brain was somehow able to translate the words into English. It was a side effect of the place's magic, she guessed.

The sign over the left door read ONE SPEAKS TRUTH, whereas the right door's sign read ONE SPEAKS LIES.

Will made a breathy grumbling sound beside her. "Who? No one's speaking. Do they mean the damn hallways?"

Bailey glanced at him. "So, you can read those things too, huh? That sure as hell isn't the Roman alphabet, but the temple seems to process it in a way our minds can understand."

"Weird," one of the others said behind them.

The werewitch was about to open a discussion as to whether they should try the room or turn back to keep searching the maze for their companions when a sudden manifestation drew their attention forward.

Out of the air in front of them, two forms shimmered into existence like moonlight breaking through the clouds at night. They were tall humanoid figures composed of bluish-silver phosphorescence, translucent like ghosts. Their eyes were brighter than the rest of them, much like the wolf spirit who'd guided them thus far. Bailey wondered if they were simply another form worn by the same entity.

They looked like shamans or perhaps alphas from long ago, clothed in rough yet splendid ancestral garb. On the left was a man who seemed darker-complected and beardless, vaguely Native American, although it was difficult to determine which tribe or time period he represented. He seemed ancient enough to have been of the first humans to wander the Cascades, whose forefathers had come over the Bering Strait from northeast Asia.

On the right was a man with lighter features and a full beard like a Viking's, but he too appeared to have come from too far back in antiquity to be recognizable. Some proto-Germanic chieftain from before the Roman conquests, perhaps, whose great-grandchildren were among the Norse raiders who first came to America from the other direction.

The dais was positioned in such a way that in order to try either of the exits, Bailey and her Weres would have to squeeze around the pair. Or go through them.

In unison, their tones harmonized like a single reverberating voice, they spoke.

"Greetings, Bailey Nordin. We have been expecting your arrival. You must proceed, but to do so, you must choose the correct path. We are the guardians of the true doorway. Determining what is true is a task that falls to you."

About what I expected, she thought. *More riddles and clever tests where nothing is what it seems.*

"Okay," she acknowledged, glancing again at the signs behind the two apparitions' heads. "So, which of you is telling the truth?"

The voices spoke in unison again. *"I am."*

Beside her elbow, Will hung his head and scratched his ear, his jaw muscles twitching as he clenched his teeth.

The spirits then separated. There was now a subtle barrier in the light that had previously flowed between them. More surprisingly, they took on the aspect of material flesh. Bailey suspected she could touch their knees; if not, it was the most convincing illusion she'd ever seen.

The one on the left was first to use his singular voice. "I am the voice of truth, and the other speaks only falsehood as is his nature. If you are wise and perceptive, the message of the signs will guide your way."

"No," interjected the spirit on the right, "I am the voice of truth, and he is trying to deceive you, according to his mendacious will. The signs do not lie, but your mind must weigh their message properly."

Grimacing in concentration, she looked again at the inscriptions above the doors.

The one that says Truth is above the left-hand door, she recalled, *but there's no reason to assume it's that simple, is there? Could be a trick. Then again, switching them around would be too damn easy. There's got to be something else going on here, like a third option that hasn't occurred to me yet.*

Will inched forward, holding his head high and puffing his chest out as though he were about to leap into battle. Bailey tensed, preparing to restrain him if need be.

"This is bullshit," he protested. "There's no way to figure it out. We might as well just flip a coin. I think one of you guys needs to tell us. If you don't want to cooperate, we'll make you talk."

Bailey put a hand on his arm to tell him to calm down, but then a blue light winked into existence behind and between the pair of guardians, taking on the shape of a wolf's head.

"If you attack them or offer them harm," the guardian spirit warned in its familiar echoing voice, "it will nullify the trial, and you will forfeit your efforts. A test of intellect cannot be won through force. We shall discover, Bailey, your wisdom and judgment as a shaman's apprentice, and the ability of your alphas and pack lieutenants to lead intelligently. Proceed."

It vanished with a flash, although the chamber remained faintly illuminated by spectral moonlight. The two ancient men stood unmoving and silent.

"Right," Bailey murmured, extending her arms and essentially pushing Will behind her. "We've got to do this through logic and deductive reasoning and that sort of thing. I wasn't too shabby at that in school, so we'll play the game according to the rules. Give me a minute to think."

The first thing that popped into her head was that when she'd asked them which was telling the truth, the phantoms had answered. There was nothing to suggest they wouldn't answer further questions.

"So," she queried, "are the signs above your heads correct?"

"*Yes*," they replied at once.

That's a start, she mused, *but it's not the same thing as a nice, easy solution.*

She pointed to the right, toward the indigenous-looking shaman and the sign reading ONE SPEAKS TRUTH. "If that sign is true and you're the liar, then you can lie."

The man did not respond.

She pointed then to the left, toward the quasi-Teutonic shaman and the sign reading ONE SPEAKS LIES. "And if that one says 'liar' and you say yes, then you're telling the truth about being a liar. Which means you're not the liar because you told the truth. But you have the *ability* to lie."

Bailey's voice trailed off as her brain hit a bottleneck, struggling with the warped rationale behind the encounter. She would keep trying to parse out the details in more clarity, but all she knew for sure was that one could be trusted and one could not.

Then a silvery light pulsed behind the guardians and four wolf spirits appeared at the corners of the room, snarling and moving in to attack.

"What?" Will exclaimed. "How did we screw it up?"

He and the other two Weres tangled with the first two apparitions to reach them, which had tangible forms despite their ghostly appearance. Bailey struck the other two with a looping chain of lightning, and they vanished in clouds of sparkling steam.

Her Weres tossed the remaining ones back and she electrocuted them as well, dispatching them to whatever place they'd come from. Silence returned to the room.

Will moved toward the dais. "Those assholes aren't playing fair. Time to play by *their* rules." His teeth were bared.

"No!" Bailey grabbed him and pushed him back against the wall with the flat of her forearm. "No, Will. It's part of the test. Distraction and provocation to make us fuck up. Just stay calm. I know I can figure it out."

Simultaneously, the two guardians spoke again. "Correct."

The voice of the wolf-spirit echoed above them. "Yes, Bailey. This is a game of questioning. You may inquire of the guardians as many times as you like, but each time you fail to choose a doorway after receiving an answer, more wolves will appear to punish your slowness of mind."

"Fine," Bailey gritted out. She wracked her brain and decided to try the simplest, most direct tack she could conceive.

Looking at the pair on the dais, she asked, "Which is the true and correct path?"

Both men pointed toward the doorway on the left. "That one."

She rubbed her chin. "But one of you is lying. Shit."

A moment later, four more wolf-wraiths jumped out of the corners. Her team was ready this time, and Bailey vaporized them almost instantly, with her three companions needing only to hold one back until she could electrocute it.

With the brief battle over, Will came up to Bailey's side and whispered something in her ear. Listening to him, her brow furrowed in disapproval, but after hesitating for a few seconds, she nodded.

The two shamans stood and watched.

Bailey hung back as the South Cliff alpha stepped forth to speak in her stead.

"Hi," he said. "You guys greeted Bailey, but you didn't greet me."

"*Greetings*," they responded instantly, then their voices separated again.

The one on the left introduced himself. "I am called Chuslum."

The one on the right did likewise. "And I am known as Gisli."

Bailey wondered which had given his true name and which a false one, but according to Will's plan, that wasn't the point.

"Okay, thanks," Will acknowledged, and he was about to continue when the wolf-spirit interrupted him.

"Have you reached a decision, or shall you face another attack?"

Will held up his hands. "Hold on a second." He looked at the duo on the platform. "So, discounting what I'm saying to you now, was the last thing I said a *question?*"

"No," said the left-hand sentinel.

"Yes," said the right-hand sentinel.

Will grinned evilly. "Hah! I didn't ask a question, I just greeted you and made a statement. You told us your names without being *asked*."

Bailey patted him on the back. "Will, you're a frickin' genius. Looks like we know which one's the liar."

Will blushed. "Thanks. Okay, wolf-spirits, we figured out which one to trust, but we haven't, uh, chosen a path yet."

They braced themselves for another assault, half-wondering if the opposition might get stiffer since they'd dispatched the first two waves with relative ease. But no ghostly Weres appeared.

Instead, the echoing voice intoned, "You have earned the right to ask a second question."

Bailey let her eyes drift shut with relief before she posed her next inquiry. "Okay, then. Which is the true and correct path?"

They paid attention only to the guardian on the right, the one who'd called himself Chuslum, and he pointed to the left-hand doorway.

"We've made a decision," Bailey announced. "Thatta way." She flourished a hand toward the doorway with

ONE SPEAKS TRUTH above it—the more immediately obvious choice had, after all, been the correct one.

Then both of the guardians lost their guise of material flesh, becoming specters of light once again, then shimmered out of sight, leaving the way clear. Bailey, Will, and the other two guys tramped toward the left-hand path.

The guide's voice addressed them. "Congratulations on your resourcefulness. And Bailey, you did well to listen to Will's idea, despite him being wrong about certain things before. The truly wise leader listens to other viewpoints since one never knows who might have the answer."

Will chortled. "Damn right."

As they started down the next hallway, which was narrow enough for them only to walk single file, Bailey wondered where the others still were. Inexplicably, something told her they should press forward. That the key to getting everyone out lay in moving ahead.

But she didn't like the thought of the remaining seven being lost in the maze. Even if they weren't in immediate danger, fear and despair might be slowly driving them mad.

"I'm sorry, guys," she murmured under her breath, "but we will get back together and get out of here, one way or another."

Madame Villalobos led the way, alert and cautious but without fear. She knew herself to be a witch of exceptional talent, especially with subtler magics, which were far beyond the crude ways of lycanthropes. One of their holiest sites it might be, but it was unlikely to have much in the way of defenses that could stop her, especially when she was supported by five others of respectable ability.

"Keep watch on all corners of this place," she told her followers, "and do not allow us to be hindered. Werewolves might be intimidated by the spirits they call holy, but to us, they are nothing but obstacles to be cleared."

Perrault backed her up. "That means no restraint, except insofar as we don't want to bring the temple down on our heads, so no explosions of that size. Anything other than that level of force is permitted."

The four junior witches smiled, looking forward to an exercise in almost unlimited aggression.

They'd gone a short way into the pyramid and were preparing to descend a great staircase when a silver-azure light coalesced out of the air before them, taking on the aspect of a giant wolf's face. It glared at them and opened its mouth in warning.

"*Come no closer!*" it bellowed, and its voice reverberated through the wide, dark space with thunderous volume and unadulterated wrath. "You are not welcome here. You defile this place with your alien presence and your foul intentions, the stench of which is readily apparent. Turn back now or face swift and merciless retaliation."

Villalobos smiled. "I think we have heard someone say that before…or am I mistaken?"

Perrault turned to the other witches. "Show this thing what 'swift and merciless retaliation' means." She sliced the air with her hand, pointing at the phantasmal wolf.

All six of the sorceresses unleashed torrents of potent, concentrated magic—swirling bolts of death in multiple elemental flavors combined with the aggregated will of the coven-mind, which refused to be opposed. The wolf-spirit tried to retaliate with a blazing beam of silvery moonlight, but the magenta blasts of the Venatori caught it, then reduced it to nothing and pressed on toward its caster.

The spirit's voice, in the middle of repeating its booming warning, crackled, warbled, and faded as the blue light that constituted its form began to break apart into a mist of twinkling stars.

Villalobos shrieked, "Destroy it!"

The witches separated their attacks, each hurling the weapons of the occult at the disintegrating patches of silver light, breaking it up into smaller and more disorganized forms until it dissipated altogether.

"Hah!" Madame laughed. "Continue down these steps. That entity should have known better than to stand before us."

She knew it hadn't been completely destroyed since it seemed to be a variety of spirit, arguably like a poltergeist, whose existence was tied to the temple. But they'd overwhelmed it with so much destructive power that it would need time to reconstitute itself.

In the meantime, they pressed on.

The soft bluish glow that suffused the pyramid's interior shifted to a dark, menacing indigo, and the silver sheen became a bright, pure white, like a spotlight. A sound much like the howling of wolves began to drift through the air. The temple was sounding its alarm.

Villalobos felt an abrupt sense of draining and confinement. It was likely that the wolf-souls maintained here had activated a magic-suppressing spell. She doubted it would have much effect.

The Venatori rounded a corner in the staircase and came to a hall of pillars and statues, where, suddenly, the atmosphere came alive with manifestations of lycanthropic heroes and other legendary souls, all of them frenziedly attacking at first sight. There was something robotic about the process, similar to the way a body's immune system sporadically damages itself in its drive to repel invading pathogens.

The witches were forced to slow their pace, but they did not halt. They were working together like an oiled machine. Their magic had been weakened, but they were experienced at using it efficiently. Arcing streams of magenta plasma cut through all comers. Their enemies' defenses melted.

"Madame," asked Holopainen, the keen-minded young Finnish recruit, "have they thrown everything they have at us at once?"

Villalobos detonated a controlled sonic boom between two ghostly werewolves, who shattered into astral dust. "I think not. It is probably like this throughout the entire temple."

CHAPTER NINE

Bailey walked down the cramped hallway, barely able to see and having no idea what lay ahead. She was confident that they'd chosen the right path and therefore didn't expect to stumble into some god-awful doom, but the trials couldn't have been over yet.

Will followed her, with the lone Silver Star warrior among them coming third, and Will's South Cliff in back. Nothing seemed to be coming from behind them, and they hadn't heard the click of a door blocking them off, either.

The hallway bent around to the left, and Bailey discerned a rectangle of pale light ahead. The hall opened into a chamber. She hastened toward it, and the excitement amidst the four of them was palpable. Electric.

They emerged into a broad hall much like the one at the bottom of the first staircase, where they'd faced the initial test. It was smaller and far less ornate, though, with no statues or friezes, only unadorned pillars to support the high ceiling.

Bailey halted so suddenly that Will stumbled to keep

from crashing into her. Then he and the other two Weres froze also, not due to anything about the chamber.

Loitering in the broad hall were seven young men, all of them familiar. They looked up as the newcomers stepped into the room.

"Ha-ha!" Roger laughed, his voice ragged but joyous. "We knew you'd make it. The blue wolf told us to sit and wait, so we figured you were tied up, but that you'd be along any minute now."

The Weres nodded to each other, called one another's names, clasped hands, or embraced, everyone congratulating their fellows on having made it this far. Then they stepped back to discuss what had happened.

Bailey began, "Tell me how you all ended up here."

The guy who'd run off first started by apologizing for his hasty action, hanging his head in sheepish embarrassment.

Bailey put her hands on her hips. "You're forgiven. Just don't do it again, or next time I'll leave you in the haunted-ass labyrinth with the shifting walls and the werebears. Fair enough?"

"More than fair," he agreed.

He went on to explain that he and the two men who'd followed him had become hopelessly lost within minutes of their ill-advised attack on the fleeting shape. They never found what they had been chasing. In fact, they never found anything; they'd only wandered for what felt like an entire day or more, through the trackless, claustrophobic maze, struggling not to panic and arguing about whether they should press on or wait for rescue.

Finally, they had blundered upon a small opening in the

far wall that led them into a tight, dark corridor that had emptied them right next to the very place they now stood.

The Were shrugged. "After that, we figured we'd made it through, and that the best thing was to see if you guys would show up. We needed a break, anyway."

Roger's burly companion, the wrestler, stepped up next to relate how he and the other three who'd been separated by the trap wall had gotten here.

"It's a pretty boring story, to be honest," he muttered in his deep, gravelly voice. "We wandered around for a little while, then we found what I'm guessing is the doorway that guy just mentioned. Came through it, bumped into these assholes, then sat down after the wolf spirit told us to hang out."

Bailey slowly exhaled and shook her head. "I was worried sick about you all. We thought about going back and combing the entire maze for your asses, but it seemed like we should press on through and beat the next trial first. After all, it's not like this place is trying to kill Weres. Our ancestors might have high standards, but they want us to succeed."

Everyone agreed.

Roger, who still had his wits about him even though his condition was gradually getting worse, added his two cents. "We've been through some serious shit. I feel like we've learned more life lessons or timeless wisdom or whatever you want to call it than I have in the last five years."

"Yessir," Bailey confirmed. "I think that's the idea. And for the most part, we managed to do it together. No more splitting the party. There's no telling what's in store for us next, and it's going to take all eleven of us to complete the trials and get back home safely."

As if on cue, a faint rumble went through the walls and everything changed. It was subtle; the quality of the light became darker and more brooding, and the smell or vibe of the place grew hostile.

Will threw up his arms. "Oh, hell."

The light, turning a deep indigo that resembled the color of a nasty bruise, thickened at the center of the hall and their guide, the spirit in lupine form, reappeared. Bailey prepared to address it and hear what it had to say, but something strange gave her pause.

The spectral wolf was not looking at her but seemed to be surveying the entire chamber without seeing any specific individual. It was looking through them at the temple beyond. It had already begun to speak, as though it were a preprogrammed hologram that had been triggered by an alarm or a time-delay.

"Brethren," it began, and the voice echoed more than usual, suggesting that it was speaking in multiple parts of the building concurrently, "the sanctity of this place, our ancestral temple, has been violated by trespassers. They are members of the species called witches, who have shown themselves by their actions to be enemies after they were clearly warned to stay out."

Bailey felt as though her stomach had fallen out of her body, but the fear and nausea were fuel to a growing fire of anger and determination.

The reverberating and impersonal spiel continued. "They have come here bearing ill intent toward our kind, and they have partaken in forbidden violence just outside the temple walls, upon sacred ground where none may assail our people. Now they invade this holiest of sanctuaries, and they must be driven off or destroyed. Let no measure be withheld, no matter how extreme!"

Bailey's jaw dropped as the realization struck her.

Violence just outside the temple walls. They attacked Roland and Fenris. I'm sure Fenris is okay, but what about Roland? Could they have gotten him alone, away from our god? Did he escape? Did they capture him? Or is he...

She blotted out the last thought, refusing to consider it unless there was no other option.

For the moment, she had other problems.

A bone-chilling sequence of howls rippled through the subterranean space like a siren before an air raid. Out of the interplay of blue light and black shadows, phantasmal forms were beginning to appear. The entire temple was about to go ballistic to fight the Venatori.

"Guys," Bailey shouted, "we need everyone together and thinking clearly. It's the Venatori, and they're here for me. They'll have to go through the entire temple to get here, but we all know they're not to be fucked around with."

"Yeah," Roger grated, "but neither was that bear-thing. Hope they run *right* into him."

As they took defensive stances, the werewitch remembered something else, and her spirits sank further.

Before they'd come in, Fenris had warned her that Roland couldn't accompany them because he was not of werekind. The temple, he'd pointed out, would react to any intrusion by another race and would not be able to distinguish friend from foe.

"Oh, shit," she breathed. Hurriedly, as lycanthropic

guardian wraiths materialized around them, she related Fenris' warning to the rest of them.

Will kicked a stone column. "Great. That's just fucking great. What do we do now?"

The big wrestler held up his hands, palms facing heavenwards. "Fight."

Shifters of the past burst upon them from the walls, the floor, and the ceiling, their shimmering forms taking on a solid aspect as they blindly attacked. Many were in wolf form; others charged on two legs as humans; and some leapt in monstrous intermediate shapes, employing the best of both worlds in their defense of the sacred structure.

Bailey called, "Stay near the center!"

As she'd predicted, the majority of the guardians sprang out around the edges of the chamber, the better to surround any intruders they might find. It was instantly clear that the spirits *did* regard Bailey and her Weres as intruders, so powerful was their indiscriminate fury. They roared and foamed at the mouth.

The werewitch conjured a ring of lightning that encircled the chamber. Almost half the guardians blundered into it and howled momentarily before dissolving into sparkling mist, but so many had emerged that those remaining posed a serious threat.

The living Weres held their line against the onslaught of semi-corporeal dead. Most of them had shifted and fought fang and claw, although others remained humanoid to strike higher, with fists and shoulders.

Bailey had not experimented much with psionic magic, but she did her best to weave a spell that would steel the resolve of her comrades, helping them maintain formation and avoid succumbing to either berserker rage or sputtering fear. She needed them tough and alert but in control of themselves.

They took few injuries as the ghostly wolves tried to swarm them, and what hurts they received were mostly superficial. Another quarter of their adversaries went down.

Then the temple seemed to learn from its mistakes and a wolf nearly the size of the legendary alphas they'd fought in the earlier chamber appeared in their midst, knocking Bailey aside and cutting their formation in half.

Then the battle became a raw and random melee as everyone strove to get back together but kept having to fight off the spirits' disorganized onslaught.

Bailey used her magic as safely as she dared, tossing blasts in looping patterns that hit their foes from behind so as not to catch her Weres in the crossfire. She also summoned it to erupt from the floor or ceiling rather than appear in a straight line.

When magic wouldn't work, she shifted, once more forcing herself into a smaller, more nimble form so as to be less of an obvious target. She pounced into the fray, using speed and trickery rather than brute force.

The battle proceeded, give-and-take. Bailey's pack was being gradually worn down through minor wounds. They meanwhile defeated dozens of the spirits, but the majority of them were replaced by others or possibly reconstituted themselves from the arcane mists.

A lull came upon them. Only a handful of guardians remained, although it looked like half a dozen more were coalescing out of the incandescent light. She thought about plowing into the next hallway but had no idea what would result from attempting the next trial while the temple was still on red alert.

Frustrated, Bailey realized that the ruling spirit, the wolf-phantom who had spoken to them and guided them, was still present in some capacity.

"Why are you doing this?" she cried out. "We're on your side. Can't you see that? Stop attacking us, and together we can *all* fight the Venatori!"

"Everything here that is not *of* this place," the spirit replied, ignoring the finer points of her questions like a scolding adult brushing off a child to lecture them, "is now a potential threat to the unfathomably long line of ancestral wisdom reposing here. The millennia of information and knowledge and magic, the precious secrets of the entire lycanthropic people, *cannot* be put at risk of either destruction or being divulged to the Venatori."

The voice's tone was loud, cold, and harsh. It was speaking with its full authority and had cast off any semblance of gentle or personable speech.

"Though it saddens us to put down our own, you too must die, Bailey Nordin, and your friends with you if that is what it takes to protect the sanctity of this temple. We must not risk the prospect of you being compromised by them. The things you have seen here can never be learned by our enemies."

Will gaped. "What? You can't do that!"

Bailey grew numb inside. She knew that, at times, being a leader meant sacrificing her own interests for the greater good, but this was beyond what she'd had in mind.

"*Unless,*" the wolf-spirit added, "before any of you leaves this temple, you survive and they do not."

The final proviso hung heavily over their heads. The spectral guardian wolves forming along the walls hesitated.

Bailey breathed in and nodded slowly. "Yeah, we're gonna take the second option. Just you watch."

Madame Villalobos did not possess the raw power of some senior witches, but she more than made up for it with her incredible control over coven-minds, particularly once she'd been able to fight with a certain group of witches for a short time and got to know their idiosyncrasies.

She didn't need to speak, and in fact barely needed to think, in order to influence two of the six to focus on defensive shielding and redirection while she and the other three continued to obliterate the temple's denizens.

"Leave!" a half-substantial brutish man cried out, bearing down on them with an axe that seemed to be made of moonlight. "Intruders! Violators! Go! Go or die!"

Villalobos flicked her hand and turned the phantom warrior to ice, freezing the arcane substance that had given him form. Then she shattered it with a sonic-telekinetic blast, melted the fragments, and dispersed the remaining vapor throughout the hall.

Over and over, similar engagements played out. The fighting was intense but relatively one-sided.

Mentally, the Holopainen girl spoke. *Madame, should we rotate between offense and defense? I get tired if I have to maintain a shield for too long.*

Villalobos frowned. *Yes, but not until I say so. Keep holding the shield.*

They had bulldozed through the first hall and come to the second, where the totemic symbols on the pillars began acting like automated turrets, spewing forth deadly blasts of silvery fire. Blocking them was a simple matter, but they created so much interference that it looked as though Holopainen and the other girl would be busy shielding for quite some time.

Then, instead of the usual riffraff, they were attacked by the gargantuan shades of what must have been the were-wolves' legendary heroes. A flicker of uncertainty crossed the mind of the coven, but Villalobos held them together and concentrated her fire on the more dangerous adversaries.

The first two hero-spirits vaporized, although they took more punishment than the regular ones. The third was stronger still, and it managed to crack through their shield, momentarily knocking two witches against a pillar and disrupting the coven-mind.

Fighting off the instinct toward fear, Villalobos created a sphere of intense sonic pressure around the huge wolf's head while also summoning a blazing fire beneath its haunches. That confused it and did enough damage for the rest of the sorceresses to regroup. With their combined power, they pushed the beast away and then blasted it into oblivion with a storm of raw arcane force.

There came a calm in the eye of the proverbial hurricane. The temple seemed to have temporarily exhausted itself by trying to stop them and failing.

"Onward!" Villalobos decreed. "Bailey will have noticed the commotion. She must not escape!"

Pressing forward, it occurred to them that the chambers they passed through must have been intended for specific activities. They got no sense of this during their invasion, though, just an ebb and flow of random hostility from the lycanthropes' ancestral powers.

Time passed, maybe stretching into hours, as they came to a vast labyrinth, which they were able to navigate through a combination of remote viewing and scrying spells and careful echolocation. Still, it slowed them down far more than Villalobos would have liked.

Monstrous bears appeared twice, and it took the witches a moment to realize that they too were shifters. Villalobos had heard of werebears but never seen one. The ursine brutes made for stiffer opposition than regular wolves. The first one ambushed them, slashing the arm of a junior member badly enough to interfere with her spellcasting. They had to beat a momentary retreat.

After regrouping, they collaboratively pushed the creature against one of the walls, telekinetically holding it there as they passed before summoning a two-meter thick wall of ice to keep it from following them.

The second werebear succumbed easily to the same trick. Then the coven had its momentum back, coming at last out of the maze and into a smaller room with a dais and two doorways with inscriptions above each.

Here, Madame called a halt.

Perrault asked the collective consciousness, *What do those runes say? They seem indecipherable and are outside any record or knowledge of ours.*

It is a trick, Villalobos replied. *A test of worth. I presume that both lead to the same place, but one path is longer and more arduous. The spirits probably want their shamans to take the harder path out of a trite desire to build endurance. Since we cannot tell which is which, split up. I will take Holopainen and Marguerite through the left passage. Perrault, you take the other two through the right.*

Doing so was risky since it split the coven-mind, but they didn't have time to check both passages. Each trio went their separate ways.

As Villalobos led her followers down the left-hand corridor, they heard heavy stone slam into place. She spun and saw that the portal behind them was still open, meaning that the one into which Perrault and the others had gone must have been sealed off.

Then, disturbingly, there was a chorus of female screams.

Villalobos forced herself not to start cursing or worrying. The last thing she needed right now was for Holopainen and Marguerite to get scared. Instead, she drove them on. Three witches were the bare minimum to confront a were-shaman of considerable power, but it would have to suffice.

"Keep moving," she snapped. "The coven persists despite the loss of peripheral members. The only thing that matters is finding the werewitch and dealing with her once and for all."

Bailey had decided they ought to press their luck by continuing through the temple. At the very least, the spirits seemed to have granted them a deferral of hostilities until the situation with the Venatori was resolved. No one had yet been into the long hall beyond the one where they'd all recongregated.

Once they pushed into it, Bailey stopped, throwing her head to the side and struggling not to punch a wall. "Oh, for fuck's sake! I can't believe this shit!"

Stretching on the other side of the bottleneck chamber they'd been in was what seemed to be the second half of the temple's labyrinth.

The other Weres didn't take the revelation with much joy either. Some slumped in near-despair; others thrashed in sudden tantrums. She couldn't blame any of them.

One made a choking sound. "We're never going to get out of here, are we?"

"Yes, we are," Bailey urged. "It's just gonna take a little longer than I thought."

There was another thing, though. She noted it, and the others did, too: noises, the sounds of feet approaching them from behind, and smells wafted on the stale air toward them.

The Venatori had almost caught up.

Bailey led them into the cluster of passages, but around the first bend in the main hallway, she stopped. An idea had popped into her head.

"Okay, change of plans," she said softly while conjuring a thick shield behind them in hopes it would mask any sounds they made. "There's no damn point trying to outrun pursuers in the middle of a maze. Instead, we're gonna ambush them and deal with them right now. The spirit kinda said we have to do it anyway, and it sounds like there's only three or four. We can take their asses, especially with the element of surprise on our side."

"Good," Will remarked. "I'm itching to let all this aggression out on someone. Might as well be them."

Bailey nodded. "Just don't jump the gun. Do exactly as I say."

They didn't have much time, but the Weres positioned themselves in strategic spots out of easy sight, while Bailey hurriedly prepped all the magic she'd need to make their ploy work.

First and most obviously, she cloaked them all. It was highly probable the advancing sorceresses had the talent to pierce through a basic illusion, but the idea was to not give them the time to realize that an illusion was even present.

Next, she conjured a sphere of lightning and held it in stasis within the cloaking field so its light and crackling noises were stifled.

Finally, she made ready to toss a phantom echo that would, if they were lucky, deceive the Venatori into hurrying after them—straight into the trap.

Moments passed, and they listened as magical combat took place behind them. The witches must have run into another contingent of guardians back in the bottleneck hall. Then the sounds faded and the mortal footsteps again came closer.

Sweat trickled down the girl's brow as she maintained the necessary magical effects. The seconds seemed to stretch to hours.

The witches were only a few paces from the corner. For

a split second, Bailey waffled on whether to spring the ambush at once, before there was any chance of their nemeses detecting the ruse, or whether to wait.

Her indecision made the choice for her. She held off until they'd taken a couple more steps.

Flinging out her hand, she released the aural mirage. The sound of Weres bounding over a stone surface echoed a ways down the hall to the right, opposite the T-intersection where she crouched.

A woman's voice shouted something in either French or Spanish; Bailey wasn't quite sure. Then the steady footsteps pounded into a full run, and three leather-clad witches rounded the corner.

"Now!" Bailey howled.

Ten werewolves pounced on the sorceresses from both sides, seeming to emerge from thin air as the cloaking illusion melted away, and the captive bolt of lightning flew up toward the ceiling before descending onto the women's heads. The dark-haired woman in the lead screamed in shock and rage.

Bailey flung herself into the fight, scarcely comprehending what happened next, except for fleeting images of two Weres spinning in midair after being caught in a telekinetic cyclone, and one witch collapsing as the wolves tore her throat out.

The apparent leader slashed at Bailey with a plasma blade, but the werewitch rebuffed it with a small, concentrated shield that threw the woman off balance.

Before she could retaliate with magic, Will Waldsbach seized her from behind, her eyes briefly flashing with indignant disbelief as he drove his knee hard into the small of her back and twisted her head sharply around. Her neck snapped, and she slumped to the floor.

Bailey shouted, "Take the last one alive! Do *not* kill her!"

She imbued her voice with psionic command, and half the Weres seized up mid-attack. The others grabbed the remaining witch by all four limbs, and one in wolf form kept his jaws around her throat, the fangs not digging into her jugular or windpipe, but poised with the points upon her skin.

The battle was over in what felt like mere seconds. They'd won, and Bailey noticed, the sapphire quality of the light suggested that the wolf-spirit was watching them.

But Roland was still in danger. There wasn't much time.

"Okay," Bailey said to the captive, her voice fierce, "do you speak English? And don't even think about lying to me."

The sole survivor was a young woman who looked more or less Scandinavian, and her strange accent reflected that. "Yes. I surrender if you will spare my life. Do you need information? I have much that you might wish to know."

The werewitch stared her down. She was obviously frightened, but not to the point of groveling; instead, she appeared to be trying to open negotiations, albeit from a position of weakness.

Bailey nodded. "Yeah, information. Start talking. Just don't think for one second that I won't tell him," she gestured to the Were holding her by the throat, "to snap your head off if you fuck with me."

The young witch quickly inhaled and then began. "Not all of us entered this temple. We came into the Other with seven. Madame Villalobos sent one back—with Roland as prisoner after we overcame him."

The two women stared into each other's eyes. Bailey halfway respected the nerve of the Scandinavian, though the thought of Roland in the Venatori's clutches instantly dispelled any goodwill she might have.

"Let her go," she told her Weres. "Carefully."

The wolf released her throat, and the men released her limbs. The witch stood up straight.

Bailey pounced on her, launching her fist into the leather-sheathed stomach and then backhanding the woman across the face. She fell against the wall.

"There's more," Bailey insisted, "isn't there? All you told me was enough to catch my interest. Now spill the rest before I flatten your head against that wall. I want to know where Roland is, where they're gonna take him, and how many are with him. Is the one witch who went back the only one watching him? I kinda doubt it."

She advanced.

The sorceress held up her arms in a gesture of self-defense, but even with her lip bleeding, she remained cryptically defiant and calculating.

What the fuck? I have this bitch at my mercy, and she's acting like we're equal partners discussing a trade deal or something. What's her ace in the hole? What crap is she playing at, delaying me while help comes? Stalling us while her friends take Roland back to Europe?

The witch said, "I do not know any of that. I am a low-ranking assistant. I am afraid that you killed the woman who would have known, Madame Villalobos. All I can tell you is what I already–"

Bailey lunged at her again, kneeing her in the side before grabbing her by the shoulders and slamming her into the stone. "Horseshit! You tell me the rest!" Her fist moved again, pummeling the woman into the wall. "You got about ten seconds before I beat your ass to *death!* You understand that? You..."

Then Will and Roger and their lieutenants were all around her, laying hands on her shoulders, pulling her away. The Scandinavian enchantress had collapsed into a sitting position, bleeding and barely conscious.

"Bailey!" the alphas urged. "*Bailey!* Come on, it's not worth it."

She stepped back, allowing them to put hands on her shoulders and stop her from killing the witch only with a tremendous conscious effort.

Will looked her in the eyes. "Hey. We need you. Keep your cool, okay? You're supposed to be our leader. I mean, how would us assholes get through the rest of this with you going crazy? Don't let this chick throw you off your game."

The werewitch took big, heaving breaths and blew them out. The words of her friends started to accumulate in her mind, calming her down and driving out the red haze of anger. "Yeah," she gasped. "Okay. But Roland's still out there."

Roger caught her eye. "We'll get him back. Yeah, he's technically a witch, the male version, but we swore we'd help you. If he means something to you, and if you need him to help you lead us, then so be it. When this is over, we'll rescue him."

"Yeah," the big wrestler added. "I mean, he seems like a decent guy. Kinda scrawny, though."

Bailey looked around and saw assent on the faces of everyone assembled. They were unified in agreement; they were *with her*.

"Thanks," she commented, suddenly abashed. "Glad I have you dumbasses keeping your cool, too. Now let's move on."

One of the Weres flailed a hand at the crumpled figure against the wall. "What about her? Didn't the spirit say we had to kill all of them?"

The girl's gut clenched up at the conundrum. The spirit had said that, but she'd also given her word that the witch would be spared if she talked. She'd only half talked, in truth, but Bailey couldn't bring herself to just murder the young woman while she was borderline helpless.

"You," she intoned. "You can hear me, can't you? You should never have come here. I'm not going to kill you, but I'm not responsible for your being in this place, either. So if you want to live, you better run the hell back the way you came before the temple starts spawning ghost wolves again, because I don't have the power to override its defenses."

The witch struggled to her feet and began hustling toward the bottleneck hall behind them.

Bailey called after her, "And one last thing. Quit the fuckin' Venatori. If I ever see you in Oregon again, or on sacred wolf ground, I *will* finish what I started here."

As the sorceress fled, the lycanthropes moved back into the maze, once more turning right at the intersection.

To their surprise, the chief guardian spirit, back in the

form of a blue wolf, was standing there and waiting for them.

"Congratulations," it proclaimed. "Bailey, you exerted good judgment by listening to your alphas and lieutenants, and even continued to inspire them when things grew difficult. And though we ofttimes doubt the wisdom of mercy, we will suspend the temple's defenses and allow the witch to flee, provided she does not betray the arrangement. You may proceed with the trials unimpeded."

The werewitch rubbed her eyes, allowing herself to fantasize about a strong cup of coffee. "Yippee!"

She didn't know what would come next. And after it all, they still had to save Roland.

CHAPTER TEN

It was difficult to say why or how the idea came to them, but the Weres agreed that the second labyrinth was smaller than the first.

The wrestler—Bailey took a moment to recall that his name was Jim—shared his thoughts on the matter.

"It's like when a woman, uh, you know, is with a big guy. Afterward, other big guys start to seem normal. That's how it is with the maze."

"Bullshit," Will laughed. "First of all, you're not that fuckin' big, except your biceps. Second, that fails as an analogy because it's about how things *seem* bigger or smaller, based on what you're used to. This maze *is* smaller than the first one. That's not the same thing."

Bailey tried not to crack up. "I'd be the one to judge all this talk of size if I didn't have appearances to maintain with you animals. Of course, if you try to explain it to me in too much detail, I'll kick your ass regardless that I'm an inch shorter than the smallest of you."

Roger snickered at that. "Oh, man! I really need to get

healthy again since that sounds like the kind of ass-kicking I wouldn't mind."

"Ha-ha," Bailey said. "Don't think I won't come into the hospital to finish you off."

In the back of her mind, though, she thought of Roland. Not knowing what was happening to him, except that the Venatori had taken him, was unbearable. She also couldn't know how many of the witches would be guarding him, or how powerful they might be.

But the prospect of finding him and having him in her arms again spurred her on, and with the whole pack together, they seemed to be navigating the maze at a stunning speed.

Their only delays came from the temple's occasional attempts to distract or divide them. It had no new tricks up its sleeve yet, and they were familiar with the old ones.

The will o' the wisps—sounds and images that appeared fleetingly on the fringes of their perception—could do nothing to break the pack unity they'd developed. None of them were stupid enough to fall for the same ruse twice, and they stuck together despite the eerie distractions.

Rounding a corner, they found themselves suddenly in combat with another werebear, though this one was slightly smaller than the first.

"*Shit,*" Bailey snapped as the monster bore down on them. "Everyone get clear! These things are slower than we are, and this time, we got the full eleven."

The extra three Weres, not to mention the memory of how they'd defeated the first bear, made all the difference.

The hulking creature was dangerous enough that Bailey had to concentrate on the fight, but it didn't take long. She blasted its face with magic while her wolves harried its sides and legs and posterior, and when it seemed stunned, Jim moved in, still in human form, and knocked it off-balance. Then the others piled on top of the bear and savaged his head until he gave up and lay on the floor, half-dead and gasping.

Bailey beamed with pride. "Nice work. You guys are improving, and I guess I am too. We win. Let's move out!"

For all that they were growing exhausted, a crazy exhilaration comparable to a second wind while running sustained them. There was a sense that they'd nearly reached the end.

As they piled into the next hallway, keeping a tight formation, their spectral guide manifested again, back in the form of a wolf's head floating above them.

"Your skills at overcoming the labyrinth have improved threefold," it stated. "You have all recognized that there is no real limit to growth and have made past learning the foundation of *further* learning. That is key. And you, Bailey Nordin, have presided over these successes. You may yet make a fine shaman."

The werewitch smiled, though she kept it tasteful, discreet, and professional. No reason to gloat in front of a demigod protector-entity.

The quality of the light and the smell of the air changed as they entered a long, straight, clean hallway. It was nothing like the shift that had accompanied the Venatori's intrusion, however. This change was pleasant.

"Hey," Will wondered, "are we getting closer to the surface? It doesn't feel as, I dunno, heavy and dark as it did."

Bailey chewed on a lip. "I don't think we're any higher than we were, but something does feel different in a good way. And—oh, damn. Look up ahead."

Most of them had seen it—a pale light far down the corridor, streaming out from a central point in a cluster of rays. As they approached it, Bailey felt her spine tingling and her suspicions rising, and she sensed the others felt likewise. It was possible they were on their way into the jaws of another trap or illusion.

Closer and closer they got, and the light grew brighter until it bathed the hallway in a stark white glare. It was blinding by the time they reached the square doorway from which it emanated.

Roger was dazed. "Goddamn. I knew a guy once who tried staring into the sun. Now I know why he was so fucked up."

Bailey urged them on since there was nowhere else to go. They shielded their eyes with their arms as they stepped through the opening. Such was its overwhelming radiance that it obscured everything in the room beyond. They might as well have been stepping into the center of a star.

Will snorted. "At least it got *gradually* brighter, so our eyes had time to adjust."

The werewitch took the lead.

Is this light the next trial? Or is it just a trick to screw with us before the real deal begins? What the hell is in this room?

She advanced slowly, feeling out her steps before she put her weight onto them. The chamber seemed large, open, and empty. It was impossible to determine where the powerful glare was coming from, but once the whole pack was inside, it dimmed to manageable levels.

"Finally," someone panted.

As the light faded, they all took their forearms away from their faces and looked up.

The chamber was long and broad and faced with smooth white stone that reflected a fraction of the glow. It was almost totally bare of features or decorations, but it was not devoid of inhabitants. A group of people stood before them; Bailey guessed ten or twelve.

Then two of the Weres made low gasping or moaning sounds. Bailey blinked and squinted.

Jim stumbled back a step. "Holy shit. Good gods. That's frickin' *wrong*."

The icy apprehension Bailey had felt when they'd first seen the light came back at once, and staring at their new company, she understood why. She had seen things like this before, but it still disturbed the hell out of her. As for the others, they probably thought they'd wandered into a nightmare.

Across from them, the figures numbered eleven. At first, they'd looked similar to the pack—startlingly so, but that was an understatement. They gazed upon perfect duplicates, exact clones. The other half of the room might as well have been a mirror.

Bailey spoke in a soft yet confident tone. "Don't panic," she told her Weres. They wouldn't be much use to her if they were terrified. "Wait and see what happens before we do anything."

She advanced two steps. In tandem, the other Bailey advanced two steps, the movements synchronized to hers.

She stopped and examined the room's edges.

"It's not a mirror," she pointed out. "The passage behind them is different from the one behind us."

Will sputtered, "Well, that's just great."

Across from him, the other Will mimicked his facial expressions.

Bailey raised a hand. "You all stay put. I'll approach, uh, *me*." The other Bailey had raised its hand, then the two werewitches charted a symmetrical path across the floor until they stood only three paces apart at the center.

Staring into her own eyes, her confidence drained away. Uncanny dread grew in its place, but the clone did not seem actively malevolent. The doppelgangers Bailey had confronted by the black pool and in the spirit realm were obviously creatures of evil disguised as her.

With this one, she had no idea.

Looking toward the ceiling where the light seemed to come from, she shouted, "Spirit! Ancestors, whoever you are. What are we supposed to do here?"

Nothing answered, nor did the light turn blue. As far as she could tell, the wolf guardian wasn't watching them.

Then Bailey noticed something. When she looked up to address the spirit, the other Bailey didn't imitate her. It just stared straight ahead.

"Who are you?" Bailey asked herself. "*What* are you?"

The clone took two steps forward so that it was only a

pace from its mirror image. "Bailey," it said. "Kill yourself. Do it. And kill me, too. *All of us.*"

The girl's skin crawled, and she heard and sensed her Weres behind her, shifting in borderline alarm. She wanted to turn and run, but if she did that, the whole pack would fail.

Instead, breathing sharply through her nose, she planted her hands on her hips. "What the hell is that supposed to mean? Huh?" She glanced over her shoulder at her crew. "Can you guys believe this shit?"

A couple let out snorting laughs. They were afraid, but by highlighting the absurdity of the situation, she'd taken the edge off their rising panic.

Facing her mirror-image again, she inquired, "Why should we?"

"It's the only way," the other Bailey stated. "Think about it. You're a threat. You put people in danger simply by existing. Not only your actions, but your power will keep attracting more and worse trouble. What comes after the Venatori? Who will you make an enemy of next?"

The werewitch grimaced, setting her jaw, and refusing to break eye contact with the doppelganger.

It went on, "What happens when the gods get involved? Will you be able to handle *that?* Hmm? You're not doing so well as it is. Roland got kidnapped. While you've been off pretending to be a shaman, the man you love was taken away from you. What do you expect will happen when an angry deity shows up in Greenhearth?"

Bailey swallowed. Behind her, her pack had gone stone-silent.

Still the clone pressed. "Do you think you could handle

fighting Freya? She's the goddess of witches, as far above the most powerful of the Venatori as they are above ordinary humans. To consider it is to invite failure. All you're doing is endangering people. Every time you attract the attention of another entity who feels threatened by you, you make yourself into a bigger target and have that many more distractions keeping you away from the people you love."

Inside, Bailey felt like she was melting, but she kept up her tough exterior. A new fear arose that she might break down emotionally in front of her Weres.

Before she could respond, the mirror image continued its pitiless assault. "You can't be everywhere at once, so you can't save everyone. Even the old gods can't do that. And it *will* come down to that, Bailey. There is no escape from having to make a choice between you and your loved ones.

"What other option do you have? Killing yourself is the only way. It's the best plan. Your death will spare everyone you care about."

The spiel concluded, and Bailey's reflection stared at her with a flat, neutral expression. It had made a perfectly logical argument.

The werewitch shut her eyes. The doppelganger was right. By destroying herself, Bailey could guarantee that the people and beings who hated and feared her would stop threatening her town, her friends, and her family. There would be no more collateral damage.

It was safe. But was it right?

Fucking shitty-ass hell, she grated. *I didn't come all the way through this crap just to find out that the ultimate answer to everything is to do what any idiot can do and jump off a bridge.*

Who do they think they are to tell me that? Besides, they're still after all lycanthropes, not just me.

She puffed up her chest and pointed at the clone.

"All right, we're gonna go right down the list," she began. "I hope everyone's listening."

The hall was silent except for her voice.

"First of all," she insisted, "we don't know that witch told the truth, but let's be generous and say she did. So, Roland's been taken by the Venatori, whatever. My alphas, my friends, and these good Weres behind me all gave their oaths that they'd be loyal and agreed that they'd help me get him back. They believe in what I can accomplish when I've got him by my side, so I think we got that one covered."

Having said that out loud, she was feeling better already.

She continued, "I can't dismiss that loyalty by throwing myself on a sword just to get rid of the *chance* that I'll screw things up. They're looking to me to lead them. I have to meet them halfway by trying to get it right, no matter what. Running away from the responsibility I've already taken on would be the easy way out. The coward's way out.

"And third, if I kill myself, then it's like saying that all this has been for nothing. It ends the chance that we'll fail, but also the chance that we'll succeed. We're stronger together. I believe in their abilities as well as my own. Not gonna cast a vote of no confidence in their ability to help me, or say they were wrong to support me. These guys here in the room, but also the alphas and shamans of the past, and all the wisdom they've built up over the years. And Fenris, our god. Would he have invested in me like this if I was doomed to just make things worse? Besides, they're killing all Weres, not just me. You think that's gonna just stop?"

The image before her flickered around the edges, and the bright light in the ivory chamber pulsed with uncertainty.

"No," Bailey stated, "we're not gonna do it like that. We'll find a way. Or push comes to shove and all else fails, I'll do it myself. Fuck this test, fuck you copycat assholes, and fuck the witches and even their goddess. We can do it because since we've been in this temple, we've learned how much stronger I am when I've got them by my side. And how much stronger they are with me leading them. That counts for something, dammit. So far, there's nothing we haven't been able to conquer."

The ten werewolves had begun walking forward to join her.

"So," she concluded, spreading her arms in a taunting pose, "if you want me dead, you're welcome to come do it your fucking self."

Will was beside her, and the others came up on her flanks, backing her up.

The eleven clones stared, then blinked. Then they attacked.

CHAPTER ELEVEN

The barn lay a stone's throw beyond the edge of the forest, at the rear of an emerald field of tall grass that swayed in the breeze that swept down from the mountains. A single dirt road connected the property to the outskirts of Greenhearth, and the farmhouse at the other end of the field was abandoned.

Within the barn, four women dressed head to toe in leather stood around a sturdy wooden post, looking at the man who hung from it.

He was slender but had a respectable helping of lean muscle, on the taller side, and pale, and his blond hair hung over his face in a sweaty, dirty, disheveled mass. His arms were suspended over his head, and shackles bound his wrists to the post. His legs were folded under him at the knees. Chains encircled his body, further binding him to the wooden pillar, not to mention restraining his powers.

Madame Pataky, who was in charge of the interrogation, slid the black leather gloves off her hands.

"Tell us," she began in her low, guttural voice with its

thick Hungarian accent, "why the girl Bailey went to this temple. What was she doing there? Why did Fenris bring her to that spot? *Tell us.*"

She had asked all these questions before, and judging by the intimidating cast of her heavy frown and glimmering eyes, she was getting tired of not receiving the answers she wanted.

Roland looked up. One of his eyes was bruised and swollen half-shut, and there were red welts on his face and torso. Nothing had been done that would kill or permanently damage him, but the last half-hour hadn't been pleasant.

"You'd make a great American cop, you know," he said, the salty, metallic taste of blood on his tongue from where his lips had been split. "I'm pretty sure the skill of asking a bunch of questions too fast for a person to answer any of them is a job requirement."

Pataky grabbed his hair hard enough that some of it was uprooted and slammed his head into the post. "Tell us," she growled, repeating the string of inquiries.

Roland sighed and allowed his eyes to droop toward the dirty floor. "Okay, fine. We were on a date. Bailey had heard about the temple, and it sounded like it had this really sexy goth-club sort of vibe, like with kind of a BDSM thing going on and lots of dark corners to sneak off into. You know how it is."

The witch's lip trembled, and she raised her hand again.

"And," the wizard added, "as for her goal in being there, uh, she has a thing for danger and the risk of imminent death. Have you seen how she drives? If she didn't have a pet sheriff here in town, I'm pretty sure her automotive habits would get her legally classified as a terrorist and deported to Yemen. Anyway, scary ancient temple. She figured it would help her get in the mood. That's how women are, needing time to 'warm up' and all that nonsense. What could be a bigger turn-on than a hazardous forgotten crypt filled with sacred mementos of long-passed ancestors and weird magical traps?"

One of the junior witches was shaking her head while pinching her nose. "This is a waste of time. We should have killed him."

"Silence!" Pataky barked, spinning toward the impertinent underling before turning back to Roland.

The wizard resumed his string of replies. "And Fenris is interested in her because she's interesting. Obviously. I keep her around because convenient booty calls are hard to find. That's what girlfriends are for, right? Ha." He flashed them his most charming grin. "Especially ones that on her end of the bargain, fulfill her bizarre kink for forbidden love affairs with witches. Male witches. Like me. It's your classic Romeo and Juliet dynamic, except that we're both legal adults and haven't killed ourselves yet. Still, Shakespeare would be proud."

Madame Pataky was still listening, but only half her attention was devoted to the task. She'd taken a metal rod out of a holster at her hip and was fitting a rubber grip to the handle.

Roland cleared his throat and shook the hair from his eyes. "Which brings us at last to what I'm getting out of the relationship. Well, I don't know. Relationships never make much sense. Maybe I've always had a secret fur kink? Not that we've had sex while she's in wolf form—*yet*—but it's something to think about. I guess I'm just a freak in general."

He shrugged his shoulders to the best of his ability with his hands fastened over his head.

Disappointingly, Pataky didn't look amused. She raised the metal rod.

"Um, so," Roland queried, "does this mean–"

The baton struck him across the jaw, creating a hairline fracture in the bone and drawing blood. Before he could even spit, she jammed the point into his side and unleashed a low-level electrical current. It was still enough to set his whole body shaking and his muscles seizing up.

The sorceress retracted the device. "Keep your mouth shut," she demanded, "unless you have useful things to say. Give us real information now, or we will remove your ability to talk."

He shuddered and shook the sweat off his face. "Oh, fuck off. What is it with witches? If you want me to spill all the beans, you'll have to torture me harder. Like I said, I'm a freak."

Madame Pataky motioned for her aides to move in closer, to hold the wizard down.

"As you wish," she said.

The doppelganger's hands shot out, clamping around Bailey's throat as the other clones surged past their leader to the sides, engaging the rest of the wolf pack in a melee that was, in every conceivable way, a perfect match.

At other times, Bailey might have been terrified. The

double before her was the best replica of her own face she'd seen, and after the eerie placidity of the scene they'd recently been through, the creature's sudden murderous rage was worse still.

But after all she'd been through in the temple, and after delivering a speech in which she'd promised not to give up, she refused to be intimidated.

She flexed her neck to protect her throat from the grasping hands, then lunged out with her fist. The knuckles struck the clone on the jaw and knocked the mirror-face aside with enough force that the hands released Bailey's throat and the familiar body was forced back two steps.

To the sides and behind her, the remaining ten werewolves crashed into their doubles, the scene playing out like a bizarre bout of shadow boxing as identical pairs attacked one another with nearly identical moves.

The werewitch conjured a bolt of lightning like a giant spark that leapt from her to her target, but it struck her double's hand. She felt her muscles trying to seize up in pain; somehow, the clone had taken control of the bolt and created an instant looping circuit that divided the damaging effects equally between them.

Bailey canceled the spell at once and summoned a gout of fire from below the doppelganger's feet. She affected the change fast enough that it should have engulfed her foe, but...

Her phantom twin blocked it with a sheet of frost, crouching on a half-melted platform of ice. Then she forced the frozen mass downward to shatter on the ground and turn flames into steam before hurling the mass of vapor and ice shards at Bailey. The girl blocked it with an arcane shield.

She has my number, Bailey lamented. *Whatever she is, she's got my speed, my powers, and maybe even my tactics down pat. Confronting her head-on really is like trying to fight my reflection.*

Back and forth the battle raged through the chamber, lycanthropes and their mysterious doubles trading blows, dodging swipes, and wrestling with no quarter given, yet neither side could gain a clear advantage.

Jim's voice shouted, "Switch it up! Everyone fight someone else!"

As Bailey sought to block her clone's magic and counterattack in a creative way that wouldn't be anticipated, her Weres ducked and shuffled laterally through the available space, reducing the doppelgangers to confusion before each of them struck at another's double.

For a minute, perhaps, the pack had the advantage, and solid blows connected with faces and stomachs as they drove their phantom opponents back. But it didn't last.

As a collective, the clones adapted to and mimicked Jim's strategy. They'd seen how each of the Weres fought, and the mirror-Bailey directed her subordinates to engage them based on who seemed to possess the best traits versus the weaknesses of their opponents. Big, tall doppelgangers attacked shorter men, and faster doppelgangers attacked slower men.

"No!" Bailey barked, "keep ahead of them! Beat them at their own game!"

Struggling with an enemy who seemed to predict everything they did, the wolves nonetheless changed up their tactics again and again, the entire battle becoming a breathless and fluid chess game.

Without warning, Bailey's clone sprang back in a defensive retreat, throwing up its arms with hands outspread. Steamy white fog shot up from the floor and the blinding light returned, reflecting off the mist and showing phantasmal images much like a movie screen.

Bailey hesitated, and the fighting paused as everyone gazed at the sorcerous light show.

"Look," the other werewitch insisted, "look and see what's happening right now!"

In the center of the mist was Roland. He was tied to a tree in a dark, foreboding place, surrounded by a dozen witches who were torturing him. Blood ran down his face and bare torso, and he writhed and bucked, screaming for mercy or rescue. The Venatori just laughed and continued to cut and burn and beat him, gradually tearing him apart.

"No," Bailey gasped. "That's not real. That is a goddamn lie."

The torment continued, the witches smirking gleefully at the wizard's pain and seeming eager for him to succumb to death. He opened his mouth wider and shouted, "Why did she leave me? Why couldn't she have gotten back sooner? She could have..."

Then a sorceress lashed him with a barbed whip, and he shrieked again.

Bailey exerted all the will she possessed to keep herself from covering her eyes. The young Venatori recruit she'd released had claimed they'd captured Roland, so the scenario was disturbingly plausible, but she couldn't believe it was true.

"*Bullshit!* Cut that out and fight fair." She was on the verge of charging through the glowing fog and taking the clone's head off with one punch.

"No, Bailey," her doppelganger retorted, "it's true. Roland suffers because of you. Those are the stakes; that is what you are causing to happen. Lives are in danger, including that of the man you love. And not *only* him. Is this what you want?"

She sensed fear spreading through her Weres. None of them were immune to the implied threat to their families and friends.

The spectral cinematic shifted then and displayed an old farmhouse—the Nordin residence. Around the periphery of the scene, dark figures were closing in.

The clone continued her taunting questions. "Can you afford to love and care about people if you insist on taking the hazardous path to being a shaman, a leader, and a werewitch? What if, while you pursue personal advancement and glory, the Venatori finish off your boyfriend and move on to your brothers?"

Jacob, Russell, and Kurt appeared, lounging unaware in the living room and watching TV, when blasts of magic came through the front window. There was too much smoke and debris to see what happened next, but she heard her brothers screaming in fear and pain and saw more flashes of menacing light.

"The witch cult has tried to attack your loved ones before," the false Bailey added, "and it can happen again. Luck alone saved some of them last time, didn't it?"

Again the images changed. The mists disclosed a building—an auto shop resting partway up a hill from

Greenhearth's main road. Gunney's business, more his home than his actual house. It was crumbling and engulfed in flames; anyone who'd been inside it was dead.

Bailey raised her fists before her. "Goddammit. Let them try! They've already fucked with Greenhearth, and it didn't go well for them, did it? Us Weres might have kicked their asses even without help from the Agency. And I think we've wasted enough time in this fuckin' room talking to you. Time to get back home, so stand aside or get knocked aside. You hear?"

The fog wavered and dimmed, then it grew thinner in the middle. That was all the invitation Bailey needed.

She pounced through it and drove her fist into the doppelganger's nose. Her double yowled and fell back toward the rear wall, and in time with the cry, the other lycanthropes roared and charged. Half the other clones joined their leader in being driven back or flattened on the spot.

Bailey pressed her advantage. "Only way to go is *forward*. Right now, that means *through* your ass!"

Her doppelganger tried a crouching, circular attack, sweeping to the side and making a vicious clawed-hand swipe at her groin. But Bailey had expected something like this since it was what she would have done in the same situation, so she brought her leg up in a crude but effective roundhouse kick. Her shin connected with the other Bailey's head and bowled her over, sending the creature rolling backward.

The clone pack had re-adapted to the Weres' furious charge, alternating between crafty dodging moves and equally ferocious counters, which slowed the advance. Two of the doubles, including Will's, were down for the count. The mirror pack was outnumbered.

Bailey's movements became automatic, her body fighting of its own accord as her thoughts and passions turned to Roland in danger, to the trust she had in her companions and mentors, and to her growing confidence in herself. Her duel with her double became a blur in which the adversary landed a couple of glancing blows but Bailey pummeled her twice for each one.

Before the werewitch knew it, the mirror army collapsed as one, letting out a synchronized groaning sigh like the rising of wind over a field, and all eleven were consumed in a blaze of white light. Then they were gone, and the true wolves stood alone in the ivory chamber.

"Gods," Will panted, "we did it." He swallowed, his emotions paralyzed as the full horror of brawling with himself overcame him, though the relief of victory made it easier to cope with.

Bailey wiped sweat from her face. "That we did. Believe it or not, this is the *third* time I've had to fight–"

Blue light solidified near the center of the ceiling much faster than it had before as the guardian wolf spirit returned in a fashion that was less like a thickening mist and more like an upswell of flame.

"Congratulations!" it said again, although its tone was different, like a clear trumpet. "You have triumphed over your inner fears and doubts, refusing to succumb to despair even when told that catastrophe is guaranteed unless you destroy yourself. That requires resilience, courage, clarity of perception, and a level of wisdom beyond your years."

Bailey noted abruptly that there was no exit at the rear of the white room.

Is this it? The end of the trial, the last thing that needed to be done? I hope we don't have to walk all the way back.

"You all have fought bravely," the spirit went on, "and you, Bailey, have the makings of a great shaman. Throughout the trials, you have believed in yourself, as well as the abilities and unity of your fellows. You've demonstrated that you know who to trust and when, and how to weigh trust in your own judgment against the accumulated lessons of the past—both the ancestral past of our kind and your recent experiences. That is what it means to be a shaman. It is beyond our purview to bestow that title upon you, but you are well on your way. Receive now our gift."

A bluish-silver sparkle appeared on the guardian's forehead, then drifted down to Bailey's face. Although it was bright, it didn't hurt her eyes, and her body absorbed it with a shudder of both cold and pleasing warmth.

The wolf spirit concluded with, "The high magic is a gift—a true blessing, something precious and exceptional. You possess a conduit to the shamans of the past, as all shamans of the present must. They can bring clarity to your visions and help open pathways to new sources of power in times of great need. I hope you use it well, Bailey Nordin. At last, I bid you farewell and good luck!"

As if a miniature star had erupted within its form, the blue light grew brighter, intensifying to pure silver-white, engulfing the eleven Weres as they shielded their eyes and cried out in alarm. Then there came a cold, dizzy sensation that lasted a second or less.

Remembering to exhale, Bailey lowered her arm from her face. To her sides and over her head was the arch of the temple's entrance, and in front of her was the clearing in the sacred forest. A tall hooded figure stood beyond the misty barrier, looking at her.

"Fenris!" she cried, relief and triumph warring with each other for supremacy in her mind. Beside and behind her, the ten young men who'd gone through so much to help her through the trials laughed and cheered. It was over. They'd won.

Their god beckoned to them, and his grim face held the shadow of a smile.

Bailey ran across the sward, the others following. Fenris parted the enchanted mist, so they were able to trot through, one at a time. Once everyone was safely past, the girl almost jumped at the shaman, embracing him.

"Bailey," he said softly, "I knew you would succeed. I knew it. But there's something you have to know."

She was way ahead of him. "Roland. One of the witches said they captured him. Is it true?"

With a slow, deliberate motion, he nodded. "Yes, I'm afraid so. I could not intervene. They've discovered my identity; I knew it wouldn't remain a secret for long. At this point, any direct action by me against them would draw Freya and the other gods into the conflict, escalating it to a level of destructiveness that might threaten the entire world."

She squeezed her eyes shut, half-wanting to scream at him that he should have helped the wizard anyway, but the mature and responsible part of her—the part that had passed the trials of a shaman—knew he was right.

"We've got to find him and save him," she stated simply. "The whole last part of the tests, I had him in the back of my mind, to the point that I could barely concentrate. I am so goddamn worried. He…I, uh," she stammered, "we're *together*. I care about him so much."

Will, Roger, and the other Weres standing paces away heard everything she said. Well, they'd heard it from the clone, but now the cat was officially out of the bag.

The tall shaman's mouth moved in acknowledgment, and he placed a large hand atop her head.

"I am not surprised, and it is all right. Let's return to your world, then. Again, I can't aid you directly, but I will offer support as far as I can. And encouragement. Bailey, if you can complete these trials that have defeated many candidates, you can rescue Roland and your town. I have the utmost faith in you."

She gave him one last squeeze, then stood up straight. "Thanks, truly. But I don't have time to soak up praise, appreciated though it is. Let's get moving."

CHAPTER TWELVE

A doorway of subtly luminescent liquid, like a bathtub of melted amethysts, opened vertically on a wooded ridge overlooking the Nordin household, not far from where Fenris as Marcus had lived for a while in his off-the-grid shack. Out of the portal stepped the deity, along with eleven werewolves.

"Well," Bailey quipped at once, feeling a small surge of relief, "at least they didn't burn my house down yet. That's good."

Before anyone could stop her or suggest they approach at a cautious pace, she flung herself down the ridge, running at full speed or jumping and floating magically as needed.

Three or four voices cried out in alarm behind her, then they all followed her lead. Most remained on two legs, but a few shifted to four. They'd catch up quickly enough.

It took Bailey only a minute or so to reach her backyard. As she came up on the pole barn, she allowed herself to half-fall against it while clapping her hands to its walls, hoping to rouse Roland if by some chance he was there. No sound came in response.

She turned to the house as the first of her pack entered the yard. The back door opened and Jacob stood there, blinking.

"Bailey? Why the hell did you go beating on the pole barn?" He furrowed his brow, perplexed.

She answered him and asked a question of her own in the space of one short sentence. "Where's Roland?"

Jacob shrugged. "Last I saw or heard, he was with you. He hasn't been back here. Is he okay?"

She grimaced as she strode across the grass. "Truth be told, probably not. You-know-who might have captured him while we were doing our thing. By the way, I passed the trials. But right now, finding him is my top priority."

Russell and Kurt appeared as Jacob adjusted to the new information. She'd pulled them all out of a recreational activity they were probably hoping wouldn't be interrupted by stuff like this, but they were still her brothers, and they'd help her if they could.

The Nordin boys all made phone calls to establishments in town or to people they knew, especially to guys who were patrolling the town since they'd have been the first ones to notice any suspicious comings and goings. But pressing them turned up nothing.

Meanwhile, Bailey and the other Weres took turns having a drink of water and using the bathroom. Being back in the real world, they suddenly found their physical needs demanding attention again. Everyone was hungry as well, but there wasn't time to eat.

They convened in the living room.

"All right," Bailey addressed them, "I'm gonna take these guys to fan out across the valley and look for anything that might lead us to Roland. The Venatori might not have set foot in town and instead warped straight to the boonies. After the shit they pulled, they couldn't expect a warm welcome. It's also possible they're in disguise."

Roger suggested he and his pack head north. That was the direction they were from, and they knew the area. They could comb the mountains and woods up to Washington and report back.

The werewitch agreed. "If you find nothing, go home. You've done plenty to help me. I may need your help again sometime, by the way."

Jim, the burly lieutenant, asserted, "And you'll have it. We pledged loyalty, and we don't take that lightly."

Bailey thanked them again and dismissed them.

Her brothers wanted to join the posse, but someone needed to remain at the house in case Roland appeared there—or in case the witches attacked.

Russell grunted. "I want to search for him. I can cover ground in this area faster than most any Were. Including you, Bailey."

She flashed him a subdued smile. "That you can. Okay, Russell will search, and Jacob and Kurt will stay behind. Russell, if you do find a bunch of witches, do *not* take them on by yourself. I know you're tough, but it takes a squad or more of wolves to deal with even a small group of them."

"Understood," her towering sibling rumbled.

They dispersed, spending the next hour and a half combing as much of the valley as they could, separating into two groups before reconvening in the woods at the southwest edge of town.

Nothing. No sign that Roland had been there at all. In her growing desperation, Bailey turned to her teacher.

"Please, Fenris, isn't there anything you can do to help? You don't have to intervene in the rescue or fight the Venatori, just help me find him. You can do that, can't you?"

The set of his mouth within his stony face betrayed his sadness. "I cannot. I might be a god, but I'm not the god of witches, so it's not within my purview to keep track of their kind. Not even when it's one who is important to you, my pupil, my candidate for High Shaman. And Roland has left no trace. I'm sorry, Bailey."

It took all the strength and self-discipline she had to keep from screaming skyward in rage and anguish. She couldn't stop her fists from trembling or a lump from forming in her throat.

Gods and witch-cults and magical rules and regulations... So much bullshit, so many traditions and alliances that had been around too long to give a shit about the measly lives of individuals in the present day.

Then, parsing Fenris' words in her head, something occurred to her.

"Wait," she said aloud, "you're not the god of witches. Does that mean the witch deity *could* locate him?"

The tall man's mouth frowned in a thoughtful way. "Yes, but I don't think that would be a good idea. It carries a great number of risks, and you might not be able to restrict those risks to yourself."

The words of the mirror phantom from the end of the trials flashed briefly in Bailey's mind; she'd triumphed over its insinuations, but it wasn't entirely wrong. Anything she did could potentially bring danger down on others.

"Yes," she conceded, through clenched teeth, "but–"

"*And*," Marcus interrupted her, "you do not understand the half of it. Freya and I are not on good terms and haven't been for a long, long time. It's well known throughout the celestial realms that you are my apprentice. If she were to manifest, I could not protect you from her if she decided to destroy you. And in fact, it would be best if I wasn't around. My mere presence would anger her."

Bailey squeezed her eyes shut and forced herself to breathe while counting to ten. Not only to keep herself from saying or doing something hasty and stupid but so she could think the conundrum over and reach a decision.

"Okay," she began, "I understand. I don't want things to get any more fucked up and complicated than they already are. But I can't leave Roland in their clutches, doing who knows what to him. *I just can't.* If we can summon Freya, could you leave before she has a chance to freak out?"

The hooded shaman rubbed his rough chin. "Hmm. You would still risk incurring her wrath, but that might work. I'd suggest you continue the search by conventional means, but if you are absolutely determined to seek her aid, I will contribute as best I can without making the situation worse."

Will and the other South Cliffs had been observing the girl's exchange with the older man, listening without speaking. They were beginning to sweat, fidget, and look around as if wondering what to do. It occurred to Bailey that after everything they'd been through in the Other, meeting the goddess of a rival species might be too much.

In fact…

"Hey," the werewitch addressed them, "I think it's best if you guys take cover along with Fenris once the fireworks start. There's no telling how Freya will react to a group of Weres staring her down. I met her before once, and if it's only me, I think I can talk to her."

Will jerked his chin; it was obvious that he and his boys were relieved by the suggestion. They'd backed her up through so much shit that she figured they deserved a break.

Besides, confronting the witch goddess alone would increase her chance of success.

The pack waited where they were as Fenris led Bailey deeper into the woods, stopping in a small hollow where tall pines upon the surrounding ridges blocked them off from sight and covered most of the sky above, to boot.

Fenris motioned for her to stand facing him on the opposite side of the hollow. "Now," he elaborated, "raise your arms and face skyward, and spread your feet past the width of your shoulders. Yes, like that. I will begin channeling the necessary essences, but you must sustain them. You must repeat what I say, loudly and with great emotional conviction, as though you were trying to shout into Asgard. Think only of Roland. Let us begin."

The tall man stood in much the same posture as the younger woman, though his legs were close together, like a sturdy column. A faint purplish shimmer appeared in the air as the summoning got underway.

Bailey felt incredible power surging into her from front and back, sides and bottom, and she sensed that it needed to be directed upward. She threw it over her head into the heavens, imagining what might be happening to Roland right now, and how badly he must need help.

Fenris spoke the incantation. "Oh, Freya, Lady of Love and Death, first teacher of witchcraft and the arts of wisdom, I beseech you to come forth! Manifest! My need is great. My cause is pure, for one of your children struggles and suffers but for your aid."

Bailey repeated each phrase, holding nothing back. Though more eloquent than the way she would have elucidated it, Fenris' words were exactly how she felt.

And with each verse of the plea resounding in the air, the flow of power toward the divine realm grew in strength.

Then Fenris intoned a series of syllables that meant nothing to Bailey; she suspected they were secret words of power unique to the witch species, or perhaps the ancient language of the Norse gods. She could hardly pronounce them, but she managed.

The shaman concluded with, "Freya! Appear and proffer aid unto me!"

At Bailey's echoing of the final phrase, a silver flash lit the sky and a green bolt of lightning struck the earth in the center of the hollow. The girl fell back a step, shielding her eyes. When she looked up again, Fenris was gone. She didn't know if he'd fled on foot or stepped through a portal.

But standing before her was an awe-inspiring if familiar figure, a tall, slender woman with Nordic features and coloring. She was beautiful in a severe and aristocratic fashion, wearing a green and silver robe and crowned with a ring of leaves and ivy. Her flashing eyes turned to the werewitch.

"Bailey Nordin," she stated in her mellifluous yet echoing voice. Her pale face was contorted with a cold, subdued rage. "How dare *you*, a were-shifter, summon me to Earth? What hubris!"

Well, this is off to a bad start, the girl thought and swallowed.

"Freya. With all due admiration and respect, you're the only one who can help me. I–"

"*Silence!*" the goddess boomed. "I do not answer the calls of your kind, only those of my own children. Why should I not reduce you to ash at once? Can you tell me one good reason?"

Bailey puffed out her chest. "Yeah, I can. It's one of your children who's in danger. Roland. You came to see him not too long ago because you thought he was special. You told me to protect him. I've been doing that as best I can ever since, but I need you to help me. You're the mother of witches, so you'd be the one."

"Do not tell me who I am," Freya snapped. Though her demeanor was still cold and hard, she no longer thundered with fury. "And do not imply that you have the right to use my own words against me, or inform me of the obvious. Our ways are beyond your comprehension. I know that Roland has been taken by the Venatori."

The girl itched with the frustrated need to do something, to get past all the negotiating and skip ahead to the act of rescuing him. "Then help me find him!"

"He has been taken by other witches," the deity observed as though this explained everything.

Must be about not meddling with internal conflicts, Bailey grumbled internally. But rather than complain, she hastily sought to convince Freya of her reasoning.

"But the Venatori are zealots. They don't represent what all witches are like, do they? They're deliberately trying to set off a war that will cause tons of unnecessary bloodshed, including witchkind's. How can that be in the best interests of the species?"

The goddess held up a hand, and green sparks of enormous power crackled around her fingers. "The species must see to its own problems except in extreme cases. We may be approaching one of those, but do not presume to advise me."

"Sorry, ma'am," Bailey muttered. "Guess I just wanted to understand."

"I would prefer to avoid a war," Freya admitted. "I have no wish to see my people wading through seas of blood, their own or others'. But such a clash might be inevitable—especially if you and your kind continue to escalate the hostilities. Again and again, you've responded to violence with violence instead of suing for peace."

Bailey clamped a hand over her mouth to keep from spewing profanity. *How the goddamn fucking hell are we supposed to sue for peace from people who want us all dead?* her brain screamed. *You mean to tell me you think we shouldn't be allowed to fight back?*

Once the initial swell of rage had dissipated, the girl made ready to try a subtler way of phrasing things, but it seemed that Freya had been thinking it over. The goddess crossed her arms in a gesture that was strangely dignified and regal, and the angry flash of her eyes had lessened.

"Yet it is true, Bailey, that the Venatori are equally to blame for the burgeoning conflict, as are the werewolves who continue to retaliate against them. They view all things as a contest with only one winner, and fail to grasp that the best of witchkind may be found in those of my children who live humbler, more peaceful lives, using their powers judiciously and for good."

"Like Roland," Bailey quipped.

"Yes." Her attitude had grown softer still. "And you are sincere in your desire to help him—that much is obvious. You also have restricted your acts of violence to self-defense rather than pursuing vengeance. I saw when you took mercy upon Holopainen, the young sorceress who foolishly went into the were-temple after you with the others. For that, I shall aid you in one small respect."

The werewitch almost wept with relief.

Freya went on, "I will tell you where they've taken Roland. He's being held in a crumbling old barn on an abandoned farmstead due east from your hometown's center, and thus slightly north of the highway as it bears southeast. Beyond that piece of information, however, I can give you nothing else."

"That's enough," Bailey breathed. "Thank you, Freya. You might not know how much this means to me."

The deity held up a hand. "Don't be so sure. I know *much*."

Roland had not been cooperative, so after shocking and beating him extensively, Madame Pataky had proceeded to the next phase of the plan.

She put her shock rod back in its holster and smirked down at the ravaged young wizard. "You may think that *we* did this to you," she elucidated, "but in truth, it is Bailey and her wolves who are to blame. That is how everyone will see it."

Roland was battered, bloody, and exhausted by now. His head hung, and his consciousness came and went. As such, it took him a minute to fully grasp what the sorceress had said.

"What?" he gasped. "What the hell do you mean?"

Pataky accepted a new torture device from one of her subordinates. It consisted of a wooden handle about two feet long that spread into four evenly spaced protrusions, each of which was tipped with a curved barb like a claw or fang. He was not looking forward to getting acquainted with it.

As his vision cleared, he also saw that two more witches had arrived to reinforce the four who were interrogating him. They probably expected Bailey to mount a rescue attempt at any time.

"Soon," Pataky gloated as though she'd read his mind, "your dog-girl will arrive to save you. Don't you think? We certainly do."

"Who knows?" he remarked, spitting out bloody saliva. "Women are unpredictable. Keeps things interesting."

The witches chortled nastily at this, and Madame Pataky continued, "It would be funny if she left you to your fate. That seems like a rare possibility. But if it does occur, then you will come back with us to our headquarters. We can always use a new witch in our ranks. Even a male can make for a good auxiliary member. Like a guard dog."

Her minions laughed again.

Roland was finding it hard to remain defiant and feign indifference, but his will wasn't broken yet, so he gave it a further shot.

"Not interested, sorry. French isn't my language, and I'm assuming everyone who works there has to learn it. Besides, I was thinking about taking up shooting as a hobby. That would be *much* easier if I stayed an American."

One of the assistant witches snapped, "Be silent! You will not have a choice."

Roland's face grew grim and serious. "I'll never join you, especially after what you've been doing lately. You'd have to kill me first."

"No," said Pataky, "that will not be necessary. We have methods for the conversion of those who are too stupid to accept our offers. Others have been turned to our cause before. You will be no different."

Something about the absolute confidence of the old witch as she said it, the easy, smirking assurance, threatened to freeze the blood in Roland's veins. He didn't think she was bluffing. There had been whispered rumors that the Venatori Order possessed psionic devices that allowed them to recondition the minds of people they selected for special attention.

As his captors amused themselves with his helplessness, he allowed his head to hang back down, not caring that it made him look weak and broken. He couldn't look them in the eyes right now.

Oh, Bailey, he thought, *I wouldn't particularly mind a nice heroic rescue, although it is a bit embarrassing for a dude to be saved by his girlfriend. But they've got to be planning a trap for you. Don't get overly emotional and blunder into it. If you're going to come after me, do it right. Be smart. For your own sake.*

Once more, Madame Pataky seemed to sense the gist of his thoughts. She spoke slowly, relishing each word like a morsel of delicious meat.

"Of course, we will only turn you as our second plan. The first is to use you as bait. Look around you at this farm, at the earth and grass. It looks harmless, no? Your Bailey will not be able to see the magic we have set here. Whatever we see, the rest of our Order also sees, and from there, any other witches who may be scrying or meditating will be able to watch the show."

Roland squinted, thinking. His first notion was that they meant to give confidence to casters who supported their cause by broadcasting Bailey's death, which would have been more than bad enough. But then he looked again at the claw-shaped torture instrument in Pataky's hand and decided their intent must be more devious than that.

"Yes," she went on, "you understand, don't you? Anyone who is keeping an eye on the supernatural world will see Bailey and her shifters storm an isolated barn full of witches, where *they* have left you. A powerful male witch, beaten and wounded, used as a lure. They will think *we* came to rescue you, and that it was the wolves who ambushed us. Then the real war will begin, as it must."

The wizard balked, close to nausea from his growing horror at the plan. If things went as the Venatori intended, casters all over the world would see Bailey's

Weres as dangerous maniacs. Beyond the Order's private campaign against lycanthropes, fighting would break out between neighbors within the same communities. Wolves and witches everywhere would be drawn into the carnage.

He raised his chin. "You're going to pay for this. I'm not kidding."

The Hungarian sorceress raised the device. "We shall see, Roland." Then she slashed his chest with the fake claws.

Peering through her binoculars, Bailey reported, "No sign of the ladies. Only Roland. He's torn up, but he'll be okay."

Inside, her heart broke at the sight of all the damage the witches had done to him. It appeared to be superficial stuff, mostly, but they'd made him suffer. Her first instinct was to jump up and run to him, cradling him against her chest, but she wasn't that stupid.

Will Waldsbach and his usual three buddies had insisted on accompanying her, and a fifth man, a member of the Juniper Pack who'd been helping guard the town, had volunteered as well.

"It's gotta be a trap," Will offered.

Bailey sighed. "Yeah. Probably. But we came here to rescue him, and that's what we're gonna do. We just need to be smart about it."

After Freya had disclosed the wizard's location, she'd gathered her posse and set off eastward in her truck, with most of the guys riding in the bed. She'd driven as fast as she dared to with unsecured passengers, and they'd made good time.

Well outside the farm, they'd hidden the truck in a small ravine where rocks and pines hid it from the road, and then Bailey had placed a cloaking spell over it for good measure. Then they'd crept closer to the barn, wasting no time, but moving slowly enough to keep sharp eyes out for any sign of their nemeses.

Once the barn's interior lay within their field of vision, they'd dropped behind a slight rise in the earth and pulled out Will's binoculars. The structure's door hung open, and the wizard was tied to a post within.

Bailey looked around again and sent out her consciousness, seeking any sign of the trap. There was a vague tingling, a sensation of residual, low-level magic, but it was hard to distinguish if that meant a currently extant spell or the aftereffects of one cast a little while ago.

And there were no obvious signs of the witches.

"Shit," the girl murmured. "They must have gone somewhere. If that's the case, now's our chance to grab him and go. But if there is a trap, we need to be ready to respond."

One of the South Cliffs suggested, "We should spread out, maybe in two groups, so we can jump up from different places at once if anything goes wrong."

Bailey agreed. Then she told them to stay and wait while she made a mad dash for the barn.

Sucking in air, the girl jumped over the grassy mound and bolted straight for the door.

I'm coming, Roland. I'm almost there. Sit tight.

Then she saw that his eyes were open. When she'd viewed him with the binoculars a moment ago, he'd appeared to be unconscious. A gag was in his mouth, but his face was drawn in alarm, and he kept shaking his head furiously from side to side—the universal body language meaning *no*.

She had no time to guess what he meant. On every side, encircling her, witches stepped out of thin air, rushing toward Roland. It was as though their movements were in a video set on fast-forward, having augmented their speed with magic.

How the fuck did they do that? Bailey's mind cried out. She focused her will on increasing her pace, but half of the Venatori had already reached the post within the barn.

Much stranger, though, was what the witches were *saying* as they moved in.

"No!" one of them wailed in English. "Look what they've done to him! That poor wizard..."

"Save him!" another cried. "The wolves are closing in to finish him off!"

Others shouted sentences in different languages, probably the same type of thing.

It all happened too fast for the werewitch to reevaluate the situation. For all her quickness of mind, the nature of the ambush was too far beyond anything she'd expected to adapt to it immediately.

Nor could she tell her Weres to hold off. They'd seen the witches appear and bounded up from their hiding places, hesitating briefly at the bizarre exclamations. But they didn't delay. Lycanthropes pounced, shifting to wolf form midair or mid-stride.

A tall, thin witch just in front of Bailey turned with jerky speed as if surprised by the girl's presence, and her eyes widened. Bailey tossed a blazing mass of lightning, plasma, and telekinetic force that closed the short distance in a flash. The blast erupted before the woman's body and she fell back, thrashing and rolling, then lay still.

But as Bailey pounded closer, she saw something odd. The sorceress was unblemished, as though she hadn't been touched at all. Hovering around her was the faint sheen of an arcane shield.

What the hell? She's playing dead!

Then the other witches arrived within killing distance, and pandemonium erupted as limbs and bodies thrashed, crackling streams of arcane power moved across the field, and the snarling and howling of wolves mingled with the grunts and screams of women.

Bailey conjured two cup-shaped shields, one on each side of her, that caught and partially reflected the plasma blasts the Venatori hurled. She willed them to remain in place as she launched into the air, landing briefly on the roof of the barn before hopping to the forest's edge, all the while summoning bursts of lightning and fire right over the witches' heads or beneath their feet. One took a nasty shock but still lived, and the others were slowed enough for Will and his fighters to engage.

The girl landed amidst the trees. Her Weres were wrestling with a pair of sorceresses, taking a portion of the heat off hers, but the other witches would retaliate at any second. She dashed back out into the field, summoning a powerful wind that threw the remaining Venatori off-balance and gave the lycanthropes a moment to dodge, so they could resume a hit-and-run strategy.

One of the witches, a stout older woman, was shouting at the others in what seemed to be accented French.

Take out the leader first, she decided. *Always a good idea.*

Bailey covered herself with a shield and, calling upon her increasing knowledge of the natural world, tried to camouflage it against the background. She had no time to test if it worked, but the lead sorceress didn't see her at first as she sprinted forward.

Then the girl jumped into a flying kick. The older woman noticed right before impact, and since Bailey's shield was still active, the effect was as though she'd been hit by a moving wall. The witch let out a loud, sharp grunt and rolled into the barn toward one end.

Roland kept shaking his head as Bailey passed him. It looked like he was on the verge of passing out. She wanted to hold him and talk to him, but first...

The lead witch was back on her feet and not badly hurt. She pouted grotesquely. "How can you do this to us?" she asked with what may have been a Hungarian accent. "We are trying to help him!"

The werewitch's face distorted into a snarl. "That's some hypocritical shit if I ever heard it."

Bailey used a kinetic blast to collapse the roof of the far side of the barn, hoping to crush the woman, but she simply caught the debris magically and tossed it far out into the grass. One of her allies tried to attack Bailey from the side, but a Were tackled her, and the two rolled out of sight toward the barn's other end, cursing and struggling.

Furious, the girl turned back to the apparent leader. "Call your people off! Get the fuck out of here, or I'm going to rip you to shreds! You have no right to interfere in our business, goddammit."

The woman smirked. "Saving Roland is *our* business."

"Bullshit! He's *mine!*"

With that, Bailey unleashed so much offensive magic at the sorceress that she couldn't even see in front of her for a second or two. What remained of that end of the barn was vaporized, but her foe still stood when the smoke cleared.

Then the stocky Hungarian turned and fled, moving with impressive speed for her age and build. Bailey's instant reaction was a thrill of animalistic joy at having won and sent her enemy scurrying, but she thought she saw a faint smirk on the woman's face as it turned.

Bailey pivoted barely in time to block an icy lance hurled at her from behind. It was the tall witch who'd played dead at the beginning of the fight, very much alive.

The werewitch succumbed to total rage.

"*Try to backstab me? Try to set me up?*" she sputtered, and thrusting her hands forward, she overwhelmed the other woman with a wave of concussive and gravitational force.

The witch rose above the remaining roof of the barn as she tried in vain to get control of her movements while throwing off poorly-aimed projectiles of ice and plasma. Overhead, the clouds thickened and darkened, then a bolt of lightning fell from the sky, striking the Venatori acolyte. Her scream echoed, and her smoking body plummeted to crash amidst a stand of bushes behind the barn.

Silence settled over the farmstead. Including the woman Bailey had just annihilated, two of the witches lay dead, and the rest had retreated. One of Will's South Cliffs also huddled on the ground, alive but severely wounded. The rest seemed okay.

Bailey inhaled. "Will, we need to get help for that guy right away. Roland, too. You guys load him into my truck."

They lost no time in surrounding their friend and carefully lifting him. In the back of her mind, Bailey recalled something about how you weren't supposed to move an injured person, but she didn't think there'd be time to wait for the paramedics. She left them to the task, hoping they were up to it, and rushed to the post within the barn.

"Roland, are you okay?" she asked.

He groaned. "Not quite, but I'll live. You walked right into their trap, Bailey. Sorry, I'm extremely happy to be rescued, but they pulled some devious shit here and got away with it. You don't..." He coughed. "You don't realize what you've done."

"What do you mean?" she asked as she untied him and helped him to stand.

He slumped against her, struggling to walk on his own but needing her help. "This was a setup. They staged the whole thing to make it look like you kidnapped me and *they* were the ones trying to rescue me, then you attacked them out of the blue. And they broadcast it to the entire witch community. Things are going to get ugly."

Bailey's stomach sank, but she tried to ignore it. First, they needed to get Roland and the injured Were to the hospital. In the meantime, at least they'd won another battle.

She helped Roland into the passenger's seat of the Tundra and made sure the wounded Were was secure in the bed, then she started driving toward town, slower and with greater care than she would otherwise, so as not to jostle the passenger. Will called 911 and told them their course so that an ambulance could meet them partway.

Though worried about their two casualties, the group was still operating on the rush of victory.

"We smoked their asses!" One of Will's friends laughed. "Like, holy shit. Anybody see any other Venatori around here? No? I thought not, ha-ha. Between today and two weeks ago, they oughta think twice before they fuck with Greenhearth again."

"Hell, yeah," Will chimed in. "After what we went through in that temple, they don't seem *that* tough anymore. And there was the same number of them as there were of us."

Bailey had her doubts about the whole situation, but she wasn't immune to the triumphant vibe, and her boys could use a little cause to celebrate.

"They ain't unbeatable," she quipped. "They're pains in the ass, but we've proven that they can't walk all over us. Buncha crusty old terrorist bitches with demigod complexes and bad fashion sense, if you ask me. And they aren't doing anything that others like them haven't tried to do before and failed at. We'll give them the same option every other sane person gives to people like that—either they stand down and leave us alone, or we blow them into atomic particles."

Everyone laughed and cheered, except Roland and the other injured man. They'd both passed out again.

CHAPTER THIRTEEN

Tomi took two trips to bring out all the food. They'd ordered not only the usual steak sandwiches but also a giant appetizer sampler platter for good measure. Jacob and Russell had insisted on paying for it.

"Hey," Jacob quipped, "we could've cooked for you, but the dishes are already piling up. Frankly, nothing beats the Elk anyway. Am I right?"

Bailey smiled. "You're right."

Tomi finished unloading and wished them a nice meal, then bowed out to check on her other customers.

The Elk's business was recovering rapidly. Bailey had worried after the brawl with Nick a couple of weeks ago, that people would be scared to come back. However, after the Venatori's assault on the town, people increasingly wanted to be around each other and support local businesses while they were at it.

They tore into their food, everyone except Kurt starting with the sandwiches. The youngest Nordin had gone straight for the blooming onion.

"Gods, this is good!" he exclaimed. "I mean, for something that's a vegetable, it's like, almost real food."

"Noted," said Russell.

As they ate, Bailey thought of Roland. He'd been taken to the hospital again and was in the process of recovering. The doctors were concerned he might have picked up an infection and had him on antibiotics, and he'd also lost a significant amount of blood. No major injuries, though, so they expected him to get out soon. Will's friend, on the other hand, was in critical condition, and the staff was disturbingly vague about his prospects. He might well die.

She couldn't help worrying about them both, but it could have been far worse.

The Venatori hadn't wanted to kill Roland, after all. Their plan had been far more insidious, and as far as Bailey could tell, the witches had succeeded in the first phase.

"So," she moped, "now every witch in the world except Roland thinks I'm a psychopathic murderer who's out to get them. Suddenly the goddamn Venatori look like the *good* guys. Local casters throughout the good old US of A are going to start thinking the Venatori are their potential allies and protectors since it seems like I'm out of control. This might be worse than when people were spreading those rumors about me wanting to take over their packs."

Jacob frowned in sympathy. "No one's going to believe that horseshit."

"Witches," Bailey pointed out, "will listen to their own kind before us. Even a bunch of whacked-out cultists."

Kurt snorted. "Believe *them?* That's like having Loki say, 'Trust me.' I mean, come on."

Abruptly grasping the ramifications of what he'd said,

the youngest Nordin looked around in apologetic embarrassment. "Shit, sorry. I mean the Marvel version of Loki—the fictional character. Not Fenris' dad." He coughed.

The others snickered. Jacob pointed out, "In the myths, Loki wasn't all that trustworthy either. But then again, we don't have a way of knowing if the mythology is any more accurate than the goddamn comics and movies."

Bailey shrugged. "Fenris did say he never got along very well with his family. Good thing I wouldn't know what that's like."

She'd meant to say that in a sarcastic tone as a joke, but it came out sounding sincere, and for a moment, everyone smiled in the quiet warmth.

"So," Jacob quipped, "aren't there like, Olympics this year? Don't follow that stuff too closely, but once in a while, it's cool to check in."

"Yeah," Kurt answered at once, "the Summer ones, in Tokyo, supposedly. They're always the same year as elections. Weird, right? I wonder if there's a connection?"

Bailey kicked his leg under the table. "No. We are *not* talking about politics."

Jacob and Russell laughed.

They tore into the remainder of the appetizers and had Tomi refill their mugs of coffee, allowing casual conversation to unfold about sports, movies, TV, and stupid shit the locals had done while Bailey was away or busy. Another half-hour passed before they decided it was time to pay their tab and move on.

As they were making ready to leave, a tall man in a hooded coat came in, striding past the waitress with a wave of his hand and walking to their booth.

"Well," Kurt piped up, "speak of the, uh, god. Half an hour or so ago, that is."

Nodding his greeting to the three brothers but otherwise ignoring the comment, Fenris looked at his protégé.

"Bailey. Now that Roland is safe and the Venatori have been repelled again for the time being, I'd like to extend my congratulations to you once more. You took swift action against our enemies yesterday despite being tired from the trials. Sadly, it seems they were able to bend the situation to their advantage. However, allowing them to convert Roland would have been unwise."

She looked at the floor. "Maybe I should have done it differently. But yeah, that was what I thought, too."

"You'll need further courage, though," the shaman went on, "for what is to come. There might be a chance to defuse the violence by speaking to normal witches the Venatori are trying to sway to their cause. Some of them have always viewed Weres with suspicion and will be only too eager to fight, though."

Russell spoke up. "When the time comes, we'll fight back. They'll lose even harder this time."

Bailey smiled and aimed a thumb at her sibling. "Yeah. What he said."

After lunch, Bailey had drifted back to the auto shop. It was a slow day, and Gunney and Kevin were the only ones working. She punched in anyway, knowing the old man wouldn't mind paying her for an hour or so of helping him with whatever he currently had on his plate.

"Bailey. Good to see you made it back, not that I had any doubts about that. Did you, uh, pass your test? I'm still kinda fuzzy on how all this shit works. Been around Weres for decades, but this shaman stuff is new to me."

She smiled. "Of course I passed it, ya old fart. Couldn't stop thinking of all the shit you'd give me if I didn't."

He chuckled and fanned himself with his cap before pulling it back over his shaggy mop. "You're getting past the point where I'm in much of a position to tell you what you should do, so whatever you do, do it right. Speaking of which…" He flourished a hand at their afternoon's work.

It was an old beat-up Chevy Blazer, a '98. Between Gunney's grunted explanations and a brief examination of the vehicle, Bailey learned that it needed its water pump changed, alternator replaced, new spark plugs, and finally, the ever-popular oil change.

Bailey shook her head. "What a P.O.S. They oughta scrap this thing and buy something halfway decent. Not that I'm complaining about us getting the business."

"Me neither," agreed the mechanic. "If customers want to keep sinking money into vehicles that are basically zombies, well, that's up to them."

Thinking of how her own new car still needed a proper paint job, Bailey set to work, helping the older man with the water pump before moving on to the less complicated stuff. They worked in silence at first, but it was an easy, comfortable silence, the type that arises between people who've been close for decades.

Eventually, the conversation turned to local news. Notably, three families had moved away within the last two weeks, all humans. They didn't feel safe here anymore, not with the witch attacks, and despite the best efforts of Weres, not to mention Sheriff Browne, to keep a close eye on the town.

"That's too bad," Bailey opined, "but I suppose I can't blame them. We have to stay, though. Can't pass the buck. We just need to figure out what to do."

Gunney replied with a carefully considered monologue.

"You're right. To expand on what I said about me telling you what to do, well, I don't have any obvious moral-of-the-story type shit for you this time. I wouldn't know what to say about a goddamn war brewing between Weres and witches. Despite everything I've learned from living in this town, I never would've expected to see *that* in my lifetime."

Bailey nodded as they started installing the alternator. "It's okay. Stuff you told me in the past is part of what got me this far, I reckon."

It occurred to her that he was passing the torch. Recognizing not only her growing independence as a young adult but also that mentoring her was increasingly the business of Fenris and the were-shamans.

"Anyway," he continued, "sometimes it's good to get away from stuff you can't do much about and focus on simple things when you can. We're in a lull in the whole struggle, and people still got to drive, so might as well be productive on that front. And you're safe. That's the main thing. Knowing that, let's be content and get some work done."

Once the alternator was securely in place, she put a hand on his shoulder. "That's the idea, and that's enough. Thank you."

The hours passed at a steady clip, the young woman

and the older man trading light banter, and Kevin occasionally shouting remarks up from the depths. Finally, the Blazer was done, daylight was waning, and Gunny motioned for Bailey to follow him into the office.

She cocked an eyebrow and made a show of being skeptical. "What's this all about?" Probably, he wanted to confess how worried he was without Kevin hearing.

Instead, he produced an envelope from a drawer and handed it to her, a warm, placid expression on his craggy features.

"Cash," he stated. "The BMW. After parts and labor for your truck, of course."

She blushed. "Shit, Gunney, you've given me enough. I can't accept this." She tried to push it back into his hand.

He stepped backward and held up a hand. "Oh yes, you can, young lady. You got no choice in the matter. Suck it up."

She laughed. "Fine. Can't argue with that logic."

"Shoot to kill," said Agent Townsend. "I repeat, do not bother waiting for them to initiate hostilities. *They already have.* Eliminate them on sight."

Mouths set in stony grimaces and eyes bright and blazing, the other men nodded their acknowledgment of the orders. This time, Townsend had almost a platoon under his command. Two dozen agents, including him.

They'd estimated that there were twenty or more witches in Charleston, South Carolina right now, and all seemed to have congregated in the warehouse Townsend's troops currently surrounded. Two dozen men were the most the Agency could spare for the southeast coast. After Charleston was clear, there was still Daytona Beach down in Florida to deal with.

They used their scanner-melters to defuse the outermost ring of the sorceress' alarm glyphs but didn't bother with the inner ones. It would take too long. Besides, the current official strategy was to use shock-and-awe, combined with overwhelming force.

With their silvery arcanoplasm guns raised and aimed, the bulk of the force stormed into the warehouse, firing the instant they had a clear shot. Two snipers waited outside to pick off any witches who tried to escape.

Mostly, they died. Startled leather-clad women with European accents spun on their attackers, some tossing off spells at once. Thanks to their fast reflexes, they killed one agent, who collapsed with poisoned ice shards through his neck, chest, and stomach, and wounded another, whose legs and right hip ended up badly burned.

It was a well-executed assault, though. The battle was over in half a minute. Townsend didn't bother to hurl any suspension-field grenades since they weren't here to take prisoners. Bodies collapsed on the floor and burned to piles of white ash.

When it was over, Townsend paused for a second to catch his breath, then he called for medical aid for the burned man. The guy who'd been impaled by the ice blast, Agent O'Malley, was dead.

"Good job," Townsend told his subordinates in a monotone. "Next time, we aim for zero casualties, but it's impossible to fight a war without losing someone." His gut clenched, thinking of the Agency's first loss—his friend and partner.

A newly minted agent in his late twenties named Gao stared in horror at the incinerated remains of the people they'd killed with such ruthless efficiency.

Townsend came up behind him and put his hand on the younger man's shoulder. "It's ugly, I know, but remember who these women are. Their organization is implicated in the deaths of hundreds of men, women, and children, and these ones arrived for the express purpose of doing more of the same and fanning the flames until the whole fucking country is ablaze. We are authorized to stop them by any means necessary."

Leaving the neophyte to ponder his words, the leader supervised the on-site medic's treatment of Agent Rhine's burns. He'd be out for a while recovering, but he would live, and probably not suffer any major incapacitation. Only scars.

With that attended to, Townsend checked his phone, which he'd left on silent during the raid. There was one missed call from HQ. He speed-dialed the number and held the device to his ear.

"Townsend," he said into the receiver. "We just cleared the plumbing. Upper pipe. Proceeding to lower momentarily. Two casualties, one dead, one injured. What did you need to talk to me about?"

The voice on the other end informed him that they'd successfully intercepted a selection of the enemy's communications. The Venatori were reaching out to unaffiliated women and a few men throughout the United States, many of whom showed up on the Agency's list of probable witches.

"Damn," Townsend rasped. "I take it this means they executed the false flag operation they seem to have been kicking around in their little brainstorm sessions recently?"

The voice replied in the affirmative.

Four other agents standing around their commander watched him and listened to the conversation with solemn concern. The rest of the men were engaged in treating the wounded man, securing the perimeter, and disposing of the piles of ash.

Townsend nodded as he listened. "Yeah. Yes, sir. Understood. With all due respect, this is why I asked to remain in charge of operations in the Northwest. The Nordin girl knows me, and the town warmed up to us after we rescued their asses. Requesting permission to take charge of the situation there immediately."

Permission was granted.

"Good. Thank you. My men here can rendezvous with Agent Balfour in Jacksonville. They're more than capable of a successful repeat performance. Yes. Acknowledged. Over and out."

He ended the call and pocketed the phone, then turned to briefly address his men. There wasn't time to explain the details, but most of them had overheard.

"For those who didn't catch that," he announced, "I'm leaving post-haste. I have to deal with a developing issue in the Northwest sector—something that could lead to us getting even more feces spattered on us than the current shitstorm has flung our way. Once you're done here, proceed to Jacksonville and await Agent Balfour. Until he arrives, Agent Madeiros is in command. Good luck, and try not to lose anyone this time."

He left, relaying the message to the pair of snipers, who had remained outside to act as lookouts while the others cleaned up within the warehouse. Then he hitched a ride with his local police liaison to the airport, where he caught the first flight to Portland, using his credentials to bull his way through the airline's bureaucracy and stall the flight by about five minutes.

After all, he doubted any of the other passengers needed to arrive at their destinations as soon as he needed to get to his.

CHAPTER FOURTEEN

Bailey sat at home, meditating on the couch. She was feeling around in her mind for the "gift" that the wolf-spirit had bestowed on her at the end of the trials. It was difficult to find, but she knew it was there. It did seem that her consciousness had subtly expanded. She found herself thinking in terms of the bigger picture and the longer haul, and the deeper mysteries of lycanthropy were starting to make more sense.

She and Kurt were the only Nordins home, and Fenris was present as well. Russell was still out helping with the patrols, and Jacob had gone on a casual scouting trip to talk to people and harvest any rumors that might be useful.

She'd also spoken to Roland a half-hour ago. He was well enough to leave the hospital, having used unobtrusive magic to accelerate his healing, and just had some final tests and paperwork to go through. Bailey would be picking him up shortly.

Outside, a figure walked toward the house. Since it was only one person and they weren't making any effort to hide their approach, she had no fear of it being a Venatori attack. The footsteps didn't seem heavy enough to be Russell's, so it must be Jacob.

The newcomer knocked on the door.

"Shit," Bailey whispered, coming out of her semi-trance. "Not Jacob, after all."

By the time she rose from the couch, Kurt had scampered downstairs from his room to answer the door.

"Oh, hi," her brother's voice said. "Always nice to see you right before something terrible happens. What's the bad news for today?"

Bailey frowned as she hastened toward the door. Once in sight, she was not surprised to see Agent Townsend standing on the threshold.

"Bailey," he said, looking past Kurt toward her. "May I come in? I have information you need to know."

"Yeah," she replied. "Sorry about my brother; he's a smartass. You want coffee?"

The agent's nod was sharp and curt. "Yes. I can't stay long, though. Things are moving fast, and we can barely keep up."

She sighed. "That's what I was afraid of."

She, Townsend, Kurt, and Fenris sat down at the kitchen table, although only she and the agent had steaming mugs. Fenris only drank tea, and Kurt intended to sleep that night. Bailey suspected she wasn't going to have the opportunity.

The agent didn't bother with a preamble. "I assume you have some awareness of the skullduggery the Venatori pulled when you rescued Roland. We heard about it as well. For what it's worth, we were under no illusions that their side of the story was the correct one."

"Hey, thanks!" Kurt remarked. "Always good to know that a shadowy government consortium believes in our integrity."

"Yes," Townsend stated, his face blank. "Your supposedly unprovoked attack on them and Roland was broadcast throughout the entire witch community in the United States. The chatter we've picked up indicates that a significant number of them have bought it. And, of course, we're nearly positive that the Venatori will be coming for you again in full force."

Fenris didn't speak, only watched and glowered within the darkness of his hood.

Bailey rubbed her eyes. "That's no shock. When?"

"Soon," said the agent. "Likely within twenty-four hours, thirty-six at most. But the plot thickens further. While their largest force attacks Greenhearth, the rest of their available personnel will be resuming their genocidal campaign against shifter communities across the nation. Before you ask, yes, we've intercepted and neutralized a lot of them. My men and I killed twenty in South Carolina before I was ordered to fly out here. But we suspect that other groups have infiltrated the States and slipped through our grasp."

The girl was starting to feel cold. "Goddamn. We don't have time for this. A day 'til they hit Greenhearth isn't long. There's got to be a way to, I dunno, mitigate the damage. Head off the worst of it before it happens."

"We're trying." Townsend shrugged.

Fenris leaned forward. "There might be a way."

All eyes looked toward him.

"As a shaman," he began, presumably for Agent Townsend's benefit, "I have connections to Were settlements throughout the world. From the Other, where time passes far slower, I can open portals to each of them. If we move fast, we might be able to visit most of the shifter communities in America. To warn them, or defend them if the witches have already struck."

Bailey made up her mind in an instant. "Let's do it. But we should get my South Cliffs first. And Roland. More magic on our side, plus he's technically a witch, so he's good for diplomacy."

She and Fenris stood and headed toward the door, where Bailey put on her boots. She had an idea.

"Wait! Marcus, since the Venatori are rallying normal witches with this propaganda that I'm the aggressor, we need to fight defensively and avoid being too brutal. It'll help our story and make it easier to convince some of them to stand down and realize they're being manipulated into fighting."

Fenris thought about it. "That *might* work, and it's admirable to try. But there's not much of a way to prove anything in the heat of battle. When push comes to shove, you must prioritize your safety and that of our kind. Sparing witches is secondary."

Agent Townsend had come up behind them and was preparing to leave. "I'd rank it a little lower than that."

Ignoring him, and reluctantly admitting to herself that Fenris was right, Bailey just said, "I understand."

Before they departed, Townsend gave them the latest updates on where the Agency was deployed or would be deployed next. "Might as well work together on this," he added. "Looking forward to working with you again."

They'd done this six times, and the strain was getting to them, but a mixture of purpose, adrenaline, and the heady rush of success drove them onward.

Bailey stood at the front of the skirmish, blocking, redirecting, or neutralizing the endless waves of attack magic that blasted toward her and the village behind her. The squad of witches—about two-thirds local volunteers, commanded by Venatori—was growing increasingly frustrated and confused. They might succumb to panic soon.

Roland raised his free hand while he kept manipulating a snaking bolt of low-volt electricity with the other. "Ladies," he announced, his voice magnified by spellcraft, "you *really* ought to consider the prospect of not fucking with us. We're trying to use kid gloves here, and we're *still* kicking your asses."

Bailey was ready to unleash the wolves. "This is your last chance," she warned them.

The volunteers looked ready to surrender, but their Venatori handlers pushed them to keep attacking. The lead sorceresses tried strikes that came in from alternate directions, but nothing could break through Bailey's shield, and they kept having to dodge or block Roland's attacks.

"Now!" Bailey shouted.

Will and his fighters, including three local Weres, shifted and pounced from behind the defensive line, bowling witches over and pinning them to the ground with jaws around their throats—not yet biting through flesh, but ready to do so at an instant's notice.

Only one of their foes, the Venatori commander, remained on her feet, and she was breaking down in fear and rage, her magic coming in poorly-aimed, erratic spurts. Roland whipped his serpentine electrical conjuration around her leg, paralyzing her with spasmodic shocks, then Bailey hurled a lance of molten earth and metal through her chest. She toppled over, and her corpse smoked in the gravel.

As quiet returned, the remainder of the hamlet's residents wandered out of their homes with wide eyes and gaping mouths.

Bailey looked at the witches on the ground. "You've lost. Give it up, and we'll let you live. Is that proof enough for you that I don't want to wipe you all out? That the Venatori manipulated that whole broadcast to whip you into a frenzy?"

"Silence!" the one witch of the Order among the prisoners rasped. "She lies!"

The other women ignored her and followed Bailey's instructions to wave a hand twice in the air to indicate their surrender.

Roland laughed. "It probably helps that you brought me along. After all, I was the one in the fucking broadcast who was supposedly being menaced by you, and yet here I am, fighting at your side. Seems a bit odd, doesn't it?"

They restrained the surviving Venatori prisoner with an anti-magic cord Roland had hastily made, and he kept an eye on her besides. Then Bailey turned to the people they'd saved.

It was a cluster of small homes housing about sixty people in total that squatted unobtrusively against a cliffside in the high-elevation semi-desert near Quemado, New Mexico. Bailey had never been this far south or east, or so distant from home. The place was the last of the threatened lycanthrope settlements in the western United States.

Next, they'd be proceeding east. The Venatori presence was heavier toward the Atlantic, but the Agency also had more of its own people dealing with the situation over there. That being the case, Bailey had opted to save isolated rural communities in the peaks, deserts, woods, and prairies of the Mountain West first.

Will came up to the wizard. "I gotta admit, that snake thing was pretty cool."

"Thanks." Roland beamed. "Don't take this the wrong way, but back when 'those other guys' were running your pack, I whipped—literally whipped—a few of them with my belt after magicking it a tad. Doing much the same thing with electricity wasn't too difficult."

Another South Cliff gave him a cock-eyed look. "You fought guys with a *belt?* That's a bitch move, man."

"Watch your language around the lady," Roland responded, although his tone was relaxed. "Meaning Bailey. Not so much our guest here." He nudged the bound Venatori lieutenant, a petite Mediterranean lady who stood in stony silence.

Then the Weres of the settlement came out to greet them, thank them, ask the requisite questions, and promise they'd spread the word.

Bailey tried to take it in stride. "Thanks, all. We don't

have much time. Have to save other people across the country."

"Do so, then," an old Were encouraged her. "We're behind you, Bailey."

She smiled at him. "I'm on it. One last thing, though. We can't take these ladies with us; it's too risky. That cord will keep the Venatori out of trouble, but you'll need to watch her. Call this number, and someone from the government will take her into custody. I promise they won't give you any trouble. They're in the know about us, and they're on our side in all this."

She handed the old man a slip of paper with a secret phone number that Agent Townsend had given her.

"Wait."

Bailey looked back; one of the local witches had raised a hand.

"I want to come with you, and I think my sisters do, too. To be honest, we had our doubts about that scrying broadcast. The whole situation looked ambiguous. And now? I don't see how you could have been doing what they said. It doesn't add up."

The werewitch and the wizard exchanged glances.

"I'm down." Roland shrugged. "We could always use more help. And of course, as I'm sure they know since they're standing ten feet away from me as I say this, if they try anything, we'll twist their heads off and throw a fireball down their necks."

The women agreed; they came across as nervous but sincere.

Bailey nodded. "All right, then, you're hired. The more

witches we have on our side, the more *other* witches will believe us. Let's get going."

Waving a hasty goodbye, Bailey's force, which had suddenly grown larger, filed back through the violet portal they'd hidden behind a boulder and a couple of trees. A cold rush of disorientation passed, and they found themselves back in the Other, on a broad boggy plain with sporadic black trees amidst curling tendrils of mist.

Fenris awaited them. To disguise his involvement, he remained in the alternate dimension, not aiding the operations directly, only opening and closing portals as needed.

Bailey thumbed over her shoulder. "New recruits. They seem to be honest about it."

The tall shaman stared at the women—four in all—for a suspicious minute, but then nodded. "So be it. I sense threats bearing down on two communities in Oklahoma and Arkansas, but according to the information from the Agency, their men should arrive to help the latter very soon."

"The Okies it is, then." Bailey grunted. "Everyone ready?"

"Hell, yeah," said Will. Out of the temple maze with its lack of clear objectives and back in the straightforward real world, he was starting to enjoy combat again.

Fenris raised his arms, closed the doorway to New Mexico, and opened the one that would take them to their next engagement in Wilburton, Oklahoma.

Tired though she was, Bailey was optimistic. They were on a roll.

The portal behind them closed, leaving the Nordin house's backyard in darkness. Bailey, Roland, Will, the other South Cliffs, and the witches who'd joined them slogged through the grass, all feeling close to passing out. Fenris brought up the rear.

"Man," Will breathed. "How many did we do? Twelve?"

"Uh," Roland murmured, "I think it was thirteen. Yeah, what with the place in Ontario. Usually Canada doesn't count, so it's an understandable mistake."

Grunts and groans went around the group as they marched into the house, where Bailey offered everyone a drink of water and the use of her bathroom. Her brothers were out since she'd called them during a brief lull in the portal-hopping and told them to start fortifying the town and make sure everyone knew what was coming.

And come it would, tomorrow or the next day at the latest.

Bailey called Agent Townsend. He didn't answer at first, but when she tried again five minutes later, he picked up.

"Townsend."

"Hey, it's Bailey," she said. "We're home. Any updates on what we can expect next?"

The Agent made a low throaty sound. "Not really. We neutralized a significant chunk of their would-be combatants, but we suspect they've still got a major force marshaling somewhere, which is highly likely to deploy on your doorstep. I have some fuckery to deal with presently, but I'll be there tomorrow, and I won't be alone. We're going to beat them, just like we did last time."

She sighed. "That's a relief. We'd fight alone if we had to, but well, thanks for your help."

"And thanks for yours. Over and out."

She hung up. Then she called Sheriff Brown to ensure he knew what to expect and had enough help. He was aware of the coming siege and had deputized over forty townsfolk, but he didn't seem confident it would be enough.

"Sheriff," she told him, "I even have a few witches on our side. Between them, me, Roland, and all my Weres, I think we can put up a hell of a fight. The Agency promised to ride in on a white horse, too."

Browne muttered, "I sure as hell hope so, Bailey." Though still up to his duties, he hadn't been quite the same since his injury and Officer Jurgensen's death.

Will and the South Cliffs took their leave to help their families and friends with further preparations. They would then catch as much rest and relaxation time as they could.

The witches they'd conscripted went off to check into a hotel. Bailey recommended one and called ahead to clear them since, at a time like this, a group of out-of-town women would be highly suspicious otherwise.

Roland took a long, hot shower while Bailey reclined on the couch, trying to unwind.

Fenris sat across from her. Seemingly deep in thought, he left her to her quiet time but was available if she had questions or concerns.

Which she did. But she waited till she'd calmed her nerves and pushed the last of the adrenaline out of her system.

"Fenris," she opened. "Do you think the worst is yet to come? I do. The Venatori might be insane, but they're not stupid. They're going to hit us twice, maybe three times as hard as they did two weeks ago."

The deity spread his hands. "Probably, yes. There's nothing more we can do to undermine their plans. However, this very evening, we struck a major blow against their agenda and greatly improved your stature all over North America."

"I suppose that's true." Every witch they'd defeated or turned away from aiding the Venatori was one who *wouldn't* be coming to Greenhearth.

He looked into her eyes. "Don't sell yourself short. What you've achieved is of great significance. You've shown Weres all over the country that you are a leader of our kind, fit to be a shaman and perhaps something more. Not only one who solves local or regional problems, but national and continental ones. And you can rise further still. That is why I chose you as my candidate for High Shaman, Bailey. You have the potential to become the spiritual leader of *all* werekind."

She blinked. "I don't know what to say to that, Fenris. I'm flattered, but I'm also exhausted. If we survive the next day or two, let me get back to you."

He smiled wistfully. "I believe you'll survive. But you're right; you must tend to your home first. The rest can come later. And the storm is brewing."

Bailey called her brothers, checking on them and making sure they'd be home to get their sleep. They assured her they would. Then she went out to the pole barn to check on Roland. She'd heard him head out there after his shower.

"Can I come in?" she asked, knocking on the door.

"It's your pole barn, technically," he pointed out. "Yes, though."

She stepped in and stood by his side. The wizard was sitting at the workbench, cutting paper into strips and drawing anti-magic runes on them with a Sharpie. She was glad he'd thought of it since it hadn't occurred to her.

She pressed against his shoulder. He paused at his task and raised a hand to place it on her arm, then gave her right breast a squeeze for good measure.

"You okay?" she asked.

He tilted his head back to look up at her. "Mostly. I feel like I...*miss* you, though. We haven't had much private time together. I thought we'd get some after that battle a couple weeks back, but life had other plans."

She stopped herself from cracking a joke about how he was only trying to get back into her panties since he was being heartfelt. Instead, she wrapped her arms around his chest.

"For what it's worth, Roland, I'm sorry about that. But like you said, we've been busy. That reminds me, the reason I went up to that cabin with Fenris was that I was wiped the fuck out. I needed to decompress, to recover. It had nothing to do with you. Wasn't avoiding you or anything."

A gentle sigh flowed through his body. "That's good to hear. After we win, let's take a vacation. We'll have earned one."

"Damn right." She held onto him, enjoying the few minutes they had together before the need for sleep overcame them.

Roland looked down at his crude sigil-strips. "I never

put much effort into learning these things," he admitted. "But their value is obvious. When I'm done, we'll paste them all around the house, and maybe make a quick run to drop a gift pack's worth off with people in town. They sure as hell won't make us invincible, but they might give us enough of a defensive perimeter to ensure that, if nothing else, you-know-who won't be able to just drop a giant nuclear explosion on us overnight or sneak into the house and stab us with a plasma knife while we're sleeping."

Bailey kissed the top of his head. "That's better than nothing. All I can ask for is a fighting chance."

"Well," he murmured, "I'm not sure that's good enough for me, personally. How about, since I promised we'd spend some quality time together when this is all over, you promise to kick the ever-loving crap out of those bitches tomorrow?"

"Fair enough," she conceded, then set her jaw in determination. "I promise."

CHAPTER FIFTEEN

"Wake up!" Jacob's voice bellowed. "Bailey! *Get up!*"

She sprang from her bed, stunned by how quickly consciousness returned. Around 2 a.m., she'd passed out, half-fearing she'd fall into a coma or something, but it had been a light, fitful repose. She'd slept in her clothes with her boots beside her bed, aware that it might come to *this*. Her clock read 6:34. She was fully awake.

"I'm up! Where the hell they at?" she shouted, stuffing her feet into her boots.

Her brother's steps pounded down the hall, and he flung open her bedroom door. Normally he went out of his way to respect her privacy, so she had little doubt that the worst had happened.

His drawn, tense face confirmed her suspicions.

"They're everywhere," he panted. "They surrounded the town. A third of them are heading *right here, right now*. The rest are already tangling with the patrols. We need to *move*."

The girl had never seen Jacob like this, and fear for him almost paralyzed her. Then she banished it and stood up. She'd known what was coming.

"Where's everyone else?" she asked. "And how many of them are there?"

She rushed out into the hall, Jacob mere steps ahead of her. He turned his head back to answer.

"Everyone's in the living room. Roland made a shield. There's probably," he gulped, "about a hundred coming for us."

A hundred? She tried not to blurt it out loud since she didn't want to make anyone more nervous than they were. *And he said that's only a third of the total force. Fenris and all other gods, give us strength!*

In the living room, Kurt and Russell stood braced for combat beside Roland, who was sweating under the strain of shielding the house. The wizard reported on the situation before Bailey could ask.

"Those anti-magic party streamers have helped a little. Neutralized a few attacks, caused a handful of our guests to shoot blanks, but they're probably destroying them as we speak. And since I'm not as well recovered as I thought," he gasped, "I can't protect us from getting roasted in here forever. We ought to get out in the open."

As he spoke, multicolored blasts of magic exploded against the shield around them, and Bailey could feel ill-omened powers trying to bypass the barrier and manifest beneath their feet. She turned her arcane will toward them and shoved them away.

She motioned for them to move toward the back door. "I second Roland's plan. You three, stay inside our shields until we say otherwise. I don't doubt the courage or toughness of any of you, but this is magic versus magic, and charging them all would be suicide."

Her brothers concurred although Russell struggled mightily against the urge to pounce through the wall and crush the skull of the first witch he saw.

Bailey sensed Roland's shield and took on half the burden of sustaining it. The wizard looked sick and strung-out. He might have been well enough to leave the hospital, but he needed a week's bed rest. A battle of this magnitude was beyond his current abilities.

Kurt spoke up as they hustled toward the rear of the house.

"It's weird," he remarked, "some of them stepped out of portals in midair like normal witches, but some of them showed up in *cars*. Mind equals blown. I haven't seen a single one ride in on a broomstick, though."

Jacob responded instantly with "Shut up, Kurt," though it didn't have much force behind it.

Bailey inquired, "Did you guys see how many of them were obvious Venatori and how many weren't? Leather uniforms as opposed to normal clothes."

Roland squinted. "Don't know, but we're going to find out."

They spilled out the door into the backyard and came face to face with a skirmish line of at least thirty women, with more in small groups on the hill, on the rooftops of other houses, or out on the residential street that led to their neighborhood. Bailey was glad they'd told their neighbors to sleep with friends on the other side of town. She'd known the hammer would fall hardest here.

She also saw that less than half their adversaries were Venatori unless the Order's minions were now dressing incognito. But she doubted it. The huge size of the assault force was mostly due to unaffiliated American witches they'd duped into helping them.

A Venatori overseer pointed. "There! Kill her!"

All the casters attacked at once, and the air seemed to turn to a solid wall of magic. But Bailey increased the strength of her and Roland's mutual shield and expanded it in a dome around them, pushing the deadly waves back toward their sources. The front line of witches, composed entirely of lay volunteers, scrambled backward.

"You Americans," Bailey shouted, channeling her voice beyond her shield, "are being lied to. The wizard I supposedly attacked is my goddamn boyfriend, and he's right here. The Venatori set it up to make me look bad. Last night, I spared a bunch of you who surrendered and even convinced a few to join us. Stop attacking us, and I promise we can live in peace."

The commander shrieked, "Don't listen to her! It is a ruse to make you drop your guard. Fight! Do not betray your own kind!"

No witches fled or defected, but Bailey's speech seemed to have undermined their confidence. Their attacks wavered, and the werewitch and the wizard began to strike at them with flanking shots of elemental power and unusual debilitating spells—confusion, sleepiness, the illusion of being paralyzed. A third of the lesser casters collapsed or ran away, none dead, but some incapacitated or unconscious.

Then a posse of Weres crested the ridge behind the

yard, emerging from the woods already shifted into beast form and foaming at the mouth with bellicose fury. The Venatori commander tried to get a portion of the other witches to join her in dividing their attention, but the large group wasn't disciplined enough to pull it off right away.

"You imbeciles!" the commander cursed them. She hurled a multi-pronged mass of plasma at the advancing wolves.

Bailey conjured a moving shield that swept across the hill's base like a rolling wave. It caught the plasma bolts and twisted them aside, then passed onward so the werewolves could run freely into the fray. The Venatori leader pointed at one Were, causing him to explode into smoking pieces, but the others pounced on her and ripped her apart.

The werewitch shouted again, "Only kill the Venatori! Only the ones in leather suits! We take the rest alive."

Russell grunted. "Does this mean we can fight now?"

"Yes," Bailey replied.

Her brothers leapt, changing from two-legged to four-legged creatures in transit. Bailey blocked the clumsy attacks of their panicking adversaries as the Nordins piled into them, knocking some out and pinning others to the ground.

Bailey then focused her magical wrath on the two remaining Venatori. One she had only to throw off-balance with a concussive blast, and the wolves from the hill finished her off.

The other matched her in a duel of lightning, fire, and ice until the sorceress overexerted herself and needed to pause to refuel. By then, the wolves had subdued most of her allies, and bereft of help, she could not defend against so many foes at once. Bailey took her head off with a blade-thin sheet of concentrated kinetic energy.

The only witches remaining were the small clusters on the neighbors' roofs and a group out in the street on the other side of the house who'd held back from the main scuffle and only offered auxiliary channeling support.

Bailey motioned to the ones at ground level. "Get them! But remember, spare the ones who aren't Venatori."

Her wolves moved to obey her orders while she concentrated on the casters atop the houses. There were perhaps a dozen volunteers, along with three more Order overseers. She noticed that oddly, two of the Americans were men. The Venatori were overlooking their usual matriarchal imperative, then, to try to bring all of witchkind, male and female, to bear against lycanthropes.

Chaos reigned. Bailey manipulated magic as though bailing water out of the ocean with the world's biggest bucket, her body functioning on automatic as the forces of the arcane worked through her, using her tired physical form as a conduit. She barely comprehended the details.

All at once, it was over. Every Venatori who'd assaulted her house lay dead. Despite Bailey's best efforts to spare them, three of the other witches had also perished, but most still lived, injured, rendered senseless, or having surrendered.

Four Weres had died. Bailey gave thanks that none of them were her brothers, but it pained her to lose any of her people.

Roland was on the verge of collapse. Bailey put her arm under his shoulder and bore him toward the house while her wolves watched the prisoners.

"Fuck," he sputtered, rolling his head and blinking his eyes. "Was I always this weak? Did I catch a bug from a contaminated needle at the hospital or something?"

She kissed his cheek as she led him indoors to the couch. "You were tortured half to death and probably convinced everyone, including yourself and the doctors, that you were recovering faster than nature intended. You've done enough. Sit the rest of this one out. It's me they want, and I need to save the rest of the town."

She laid him down, gave his hand a final squeeze, and plunged back out onto the battlefield that had once been her yard.

"Jacob. Kurt," she called. "Stay here. Protect Roland, not to mention our house. Russell, come with me. I know you would anyway. We're going down Main Street to collect the other Weres and join up with Sheriff Browne and anyone else willing to help, to launch a coordinated counterattack. We've got to at least hold them off 'til the fuckin' Agency shows up. They should be here already, but oh, well. Same strategy. Spare the dupes, but kill anyone wearing leather. Let's go."

She put a hand on the shoulders of the eldest and youngest of her brothers, while the hulking shape of the middle followed her and her remaining allies protected their flanks. At her command, everyone in human form shifted, and a platoon of wolves bounded with desperate speed through the northwest subdivision toward the center of town.

Flames were rising on Main Street.

Sheriff Browne refused to be caught like a rat in a trap again. Last time that had happened, Jurgensen had paid with his life, and he still couldn't walk unsupported. The irony was that his station was meant to be secure, but it was designed and built to withstand criminals or rioters. Not an army of witches.

So he'd posted men on the roof of the station and on the roofs of the surrounding buildings and had them keeping watch all night, rotating shifts and drilling them in the protocol of how to react when the Venatori's sword stroke came.

It happened just after dawn, five minutes after Browne had woken up on the cot he'd dragged into the station.

Alarms went off, and men barked and shouted through walkie-talkies. Gunshots pierced the peaceful air, answered by bizarre whooshing and crackling sounds that could only be expulsions of magic. Feet stamped, bodies fell, car tires squealed, and wolves howled.

Browne grabbed his rifle. Slinging it over his shoulder, he hobbled toward the ladder and started to climb. Despite his leg injury and the fact that he could stand to lose fifty or sixty pounds, he ascended, and the reports coming through his radio indicated that two of his men still held the station's roof. He emerged to find them lying on their bellies, taking potshots into the center of the street. The ridiculous paper strips the Seattle kid had gifted them with last night were still intact around the edge of the building.

One of the men looked over his shoulder. "Sheriff. They showed up in a big way. Multiple carloads, plus a bunch stepped out of portals and shit. I'd estimate two hundred storming the middle of town, maybe more, and others are bearing northwest. Probably going after Bailey.

The sheriff scanned the village quickly before he dropped painfully to his knees and crawled over to join the men. The streets were swarming with hostile figures, and the sky blazed with magic. Mostly women, of course, but the Venatori seemed to have relaxed their hiring policies since maybe ten percent of the invading force was composed of men. On the plus side, the lackeys seemed to outnumber the Order members.

Browne unslung his rifle and fired a trio of well-placed shots over the rim. Two witches by the hardware store dropped to the asphalt.

During a lull in the noise, he asked, "What's the word on the Men in Black? Where are the wolves?"

"No word on the former," the nearer deputy responded, "but the wolves are already doing their thing. Look."

Squinting over the edge of the roof, the sheriff saw brownish shapes dashing out of the woods or from alleys and side streets to fling themselves berserker-like into the lines of the casters. Others encircled the main formation and skirmished with or distracted them while their comrades ganged up on major targets, prioritizing the European officers in their strange leather uniforms.

Browne shook his head and reloaded his rifle. "Not doing too badly so far, but you know the bitches have something up their sleeve. And with that many of them, if the Feds don't show up pronto, we could–"

A purple bolt of lightning struck to his right. He rolled aside as dust and rocks and burning debris rained over him. After his vision cleared, he saw that the deputized citizen he'd just spoken to was gone, and so was that entire section of the roof. All that was left was a smoking boot.

"God*dammit*," he grated, then turned and started shooting.

On a more encouraging note, he saw a massive lifted truck—it belonged to one of the South Cliff boys if he recalled—barreling into town at a highly illegal speed. The witches, not expecting counterattack via vehicle, were caught off-guard and the truck plowed into their ranks, sending four or five of them scattering like bowling pins and crushing as many others.

"*Yeeeeehaw!*" someone down below screamed. Two Venatori stepped out to blast the truck as it sped to the other side of Main Street, only for three wolves to ambush them and knock them into a wall. Then flames rose and bodies tangled and Browne could see no more.

"Christ," he whispered. "There isn't even 'law and order' here anymore. This has turned into a goddamn guerilla war. Bailey, where are you, girl?"

On the street beneath the sheriff's blasted roof, a group of the invaders near the rear separated from the main formation. They'd elected to perform harrying strikes against the rest of the town to draw the Weres' defenses away from any type of unified counterassault. There were four of them, all volunteers, commanded by a prematurely balding male witch who wore narrow black spectacles.

"Um," he observed, "it looks like some of the yokels are taking refuge in that auto body shop up the hill. Let's go make them uncomfortable. The Order said to pursue reprisals against local businesses if they resist."

"Okay," his witches agreed. They weren't overly bright, but they were skilled enough at flinging spells around.

They marched up the street toward the shop, noting that the proprietor and employees had made a barricade out front consisting of cars and trucks parked end to end.

The wizard scoffed. "They actually think that will stop us?"

Drawing on the rudimentary coven-mind he'd established with his followers, he extended his hands and made a motion like opening a cabinet. Two of the cars in the middle of the barricade swung outward, pivoting on a single wheel each and leaving a nice wide space for the quartet to advance through.

As soon as the witches did, though, they smelled gasoline and saw a guy in a dirty baseball cap duck out and toss a flaming rag onto the ground.

Eyes widened. "Oh, shit!" one of the females exclaimed. A burning trail ran along the ground with startling speed and nearly engulfed them all. The woman who'd cried out stumbled back and tripped over the hood of a car, clonking her head on the ground and then lying motionless.

The leader suppressed the flames with a blast of cold, wet vapor while the other two moved around him and collaboratively tossed a sonic boom into the center of the shop. Windows shattered, and concrete and plaster cracked. The roof buckled.

Then a giant pile of tires that had been heaped atop the building out of sight spilled down toward the trio. The wizard rolled out of the way, but the heavy rubber rings smashed into his subordinates, breaking one's leg and knocking her out, and burying the other so she lay with her arms trapped under her. Lacking the skill to perform spells without hand motions, she was helpless.

Enraged, the male witch advanced into the repair bay, where the short, stout man in the cap who'd ignited the gas trail stood.

Gunney waved. "We were gonna push those tires down on you guys ourselves, like throwing boulders off a medieval battlement in a siege or whatnot, but looks like you beat us to it. Good job."

His reply came in the form of a combined bolt of flame and concentrated sound. The old mechanic raised a hubcap, holding it like a shield, which had a couple of strips of paper inscribed with runes glued to the front. The blast vanished harmlessly.

"So," the bespectacled wizard sneered, deciding against another direct attack, "you're the hick grease monkey type who likes vehicles. I bet they're like your children. How about..."

The man suddenly pivoted and threw a rippling fireball with a semisolid core of heated rock at a red pickup in the far corner of the lot. The projectile smashed through the window and buried itself under the steering compartment, melting its way into the engine as flames engulfed the frame. They quickly reached the fuel tank.

The air crackled and a small shockwave went across the lot as the truck exploded, turning end over end and coming to rest as a burning, smoky husk at the other end of the gravel.

"See?" said the wizard, glaring at the mechanic. "That's what happens when you get in our way."

Gunney burst out laughing, his hands clamping over his belly. "Oh, my God! You don't understand. That's Bob Holmwell's truck. I hate that dickhead. Oh, man." He paused to catch his breath. "Hell, I was hoping he'd suffer *some* kinda collateral damage during this shitshow."

The sorcerer's face scrunched in indignation, and he turned toward Gunney's pickup. "Then we'll just have to–"

The mechanic whacked him in the back of the head with a rusty muffler. Making a strange gobbling noise, the man pitched into a pile of tires and lay unconscious in a heap among them.

"Yeah, yeah," Gunney muttered. "Whatever you say, pal. You'd think I'd never seen a truck explode before."

"Fuck." Townsend stood, glowering at the light show and fighting going on in the little town in the valley below them. "They started the party without us. Was hoping the Order would take longer to get their shit together. Move in immediately!"

His lieutenants barked, "Yes, sir!" and scrambled to their positions. Walkie-talkies crackled as someone told the helicopters to deploy and engage. The few men not already sitting in their fleet of armored trucks and Jeeps piled back in, then the entire Northwestern complement of the Agency's might descended upon Greenhearth.

In Townsend's opinion, the helicopters flew in too soon.

By attacking ahead of the ground force, they announced their arrival before a coordinated strike could smash the witches into the dirt. But with the whole middle of the town going up in flames and what looked like hundreds of spell-casters swarming around, there was no time to waste. The defenders would be overwhelmed without immediate relief.

Townsend rode in one of the largest and most powerful vehicles they possessed—a repurposed Armored Personnel Carrier they'd requisitioned from the military. Two men manned a rotating turret on top, armed with mounted arcanoplasm cannons.

As the enemy came within range, Townsend realized they had a problem. He'd issued a recommendation to the sheriff to order all locals to stay in their homes once fighting broke out. That way, anyone on the streets, even if dressed in civvies, could be assumed to be a Venatori lackey.

But it looked like the sheriff's order had been ignored. Clusters of people struggled all over, and moving at speed, the agents couldn't tell the witches from the normal people.

"Dammit," he cursed.

Through the comm system linking the entire fleet, he ordered, "Concentrate our fire mainly on the obvious Venatori. Avoid lethal force against anyone who appears to be a civilian unless they threaten us. I repeat, only shoot to kill the Venatori or active hostiles."

Then the clusterfuck began. He had eighty men with him, spread among two dozen vehicles, and with the proven effectiveness of their arcanoplasm throwers and static-field grenades, they wrought massive havoc on the

Order's troops. But the town had descended into disorganized street-to-street skirmishing as the Venatori rained fire and death on any buildings or people they could.

"Sir," a junior agent said over the comm, "Weres coming in from the west."

A fleet of wolves stormed the right flank of the sorceresses' battalion. Six or seven of them died almost immediately in the brutal counterattack, but they dropped as many witches, and with that section of the formation trapped between Weres and agents, it was quickly ground to a pulp.

In the sky, the Agency's choppers swept overhead again, magenta beams streaking down to burn through the enemy. To Townsend's fury, they seemed to be all but ignoring his order to avoid non-Venatori casualties and were simply blasting into any group that looked like it was casting spells.

But before an entire aggregation of plainclothes witches could be incinerated, someone blocked the arcanoplasm beams with a magical shield.

"Wait!" a voice cried. "Stop! This doesn't have to happen. You're being lied to, and I can prove it!"

Townsend blinked. He leaned out the side of his vehicle, despite the danger, to get a better look.

"It's Bailey."

Bailey raised her arms as the violence stalled around her; she magnified her voice so it echoed over the valley.

"Where are the witches who joined me? Tell them! Tell them that I never attacked Roland. I'm *dating* him, for fuck's sake. The Venatori kidnapped him and set the whole thing up to turn you against me! Don't do this, or everyone is going to die!"

She thought she saw the quartet of sorceresses who'd defected to their side over by the sheriff's station, but it was difficult to say with the streets thronged with people and choked with smoking wreckage.

Someone, presumably a Venatori overseer, took a cheap shot at her with a curved lightning bolt, but the werewitch caught it and tossed it back into the sky. As had happened at her house, it looked like some of the volunteers were half-convinced, but the fighting would start again at any minute. It was still raging in the far corners of town.

Then another voice spoke, magnified like hers, and a slender figure appeared on the roof of the bank.

"Hi, remember me?" said Roland's voice. "You might remember me as the guy in the scry-video tied to the post in the barn."

Bailey's eyes bulged. "Roland! Dammit!" She choked on her words. She'd wanted to tell him he shouldn't be here, given his weakened condition, but that would just make it look like he was about to validate the Venatori's account while she was trying to suppress him from speaking.

"I wanted to say," he went on, his voice filling the streets, "that yes, Bailey and I are an item, and I definitely wasn't relying on our friends in the leather jumpsuits to save me from my girlfriend. More like the other way around. That was setup, and any witch who's here because she thinks Bailey is out to get us has been duped. The real enemy is the Venatori, who started annihilating Weres a month ago and are now in PR damage-control mode."

The werewitch expected the Order's troops to try to assassinate him at any moment, but they didn't, perhaps because they didn't want to be seen attacking a fellow member of witchkind.

With the doubt and confusion that Roland's presence had sowed, the invading force's unity cracked asunder while the Venatori screamed at their conscripts to attack. Instead, the Weres and agents pressed their advantage.

"Spare the regular witches!" Bailey ordered as her allies tore into the casters. "Only kill the Venatori!"

The Order's pawns scattered or surrendered en masse, and with an abrupt rush of triumph, Bailey realized they were going to win. The cult's plan had failed.

However, they had a backup. A barely-perceptible noise, supersonic and riding vibrations of the arcane as much as mortal sound, rippled through the air. Bailey felt it more than she heard it, and it occurred to her that it was an alarm that could reach through time and space.

Portals opened throughout the town. Leather-clad witches streamed out, hurling blasts of death at the swarming Weres, at the Agency's trucks and choppers, and at the town's deputies and defensive militia. But not, Bailey saw, at the masses of non-Order sorcerers and sorceresses who'd given up.

They're still trying to work the angle that they're the protectors of witchkind, Bailey surmised. *We have no choice but to stomp them so we can debrief their patsies later. But the number of the Venatori in the fight just damn near doubled.*

She was about to plunge into the melee when Roland drifted down to her side from his perch.

"What," she shouted, "the *hell* do you think you're doing risking yourself like this?"

"Oh," he quipped, "helping you. And I'm about to take another risk that will finish the whole battle."

He looked terrible; his wounds were raw again, as though his recovery were backtracking, and there were dark circles under his eyes. She was about to forbid him or beg him if she had to, but he spoke first.

"Trust me. It's chancy, but we're all risking ourselves anyway. Time to fight fire with fire. And if this doesn't work, I love you. Remember that."

Before she could stop him, he'd dashed into the middle of the roiling violence along Main Street, augmenting his speed through magic, shoving combatants aside by surrounding himself with kinetic force.

He was making a beeline toward an objective, and Bailey saw what it was—the apparent overall commander of the Venatori assault, who was none other than the stocky Eastern European battleax who'd presided over his torture at the barn.

Bailey ran behind him, fending off blasts from enraged witches and returning fire when she could, but never slowing down.

Roland shouted at the Hungarian witch and waved his arms, and the werewitch grasped that he was casting a spell. It was subtle and beyond her immediate comprehension.

"Wait!" she cried out. "Roland, what are you doing?"

"Hey!" he bellowed, heedless of her, and the Hungarian caught sight of him, her face twisted in a cruel mask of anger and frustrated malevolence. "We have unfinished business, you and I!"

Then Bailey understood why he was being so reckless and what sort of magic he'd just worked. He was casting a scry-broadcast of his own. Many of the lay-sorceresses along the street had put hands to their heads as though they were seeing or hearing things from afar, and undoubtedly there were other witches across America and the world who were tuning in as well.

Madame Pataky stepped toward him. "Yes," she snarled, "we do. But it is finished *now*."

A spiraling bolt of heated, accelerated particles leapt from the witch's hands with such speed that it seemed to streak down the entire road in a nanosecond.

But Bailey saw only part of it, and in that small snapshot, her world ended. The part she saw went straight through Roland's torso, raising a misting spray of his blood, then sent him toppling to the asphalt.

CHAPTER SIXTEEN

Screams went around the square as the wizard fell, and some of them formed coherent words. "Why'd she do that? He's one of us!" queried a female voice with an American accent.

Bailey was in motion, closing the distance between her and Roland faster than she would have thought possible. Madame Pataky fired another blast, but she deflected it with an offhand motion.

Three other non-Order witches knelt over the wizard's body. His mouth was moving, so he wasn't dead yet.

Bailey stalled for a split second. "Help him!" she cried to the women, then she was darting toward the perpetrator.

The battle slowed, then melted away as she drove toward the Hungarian, unable to think of anything except stopping the Venatori's commander from hurting Roland more or hurting anyone else ever again. Weres moved in to corral the volunteer casters who'd surrendered. The Agency's men vaporized those witches who still fought.

Madame Pataky's heavy face was set in an arrogant

expression of triumph. She crossed her hands in front of her chest, and Bailey was assailed by six diagonal streams of plasma from multiple directions. She leapt over two and blocked the rest, and then she was within killing distance.

The commander hit her with a sonic-concussive force that drove the werewitch back, her legs flopping and her ears popping, but she maintained a shield even while stunned so that Pataky's lightning strike dissipated before it could fry her.

"You think," the Venatori Madame shouted, "you are so smart and brave. But everything you have done here will be meaningless when you *die* like the traitor wizard."

Bailey landed on her feet and tried to encase the sorceress in ice. Pataky stopped it before it reached her flesh, but it created enough of a delay for her to send her mind out into the cosmic depths, seeking any advice the shamanic spirits might give her.

As her Weres shifted back to human form and unaffiliated witches begged for mercy or apologized for their mistakes, one simple sentence declared itself in Bailey's mind.

You are all of us.

At first, she worried that it was too vague to be of any use, but then it gave her an idea.

The Venatori commander fired another bolt of accelerated matter. Bailey flash-stepped aside, wincing as it put a hole through a sandwich shop's walls, and then thought of how she'd succeeded at shifting into a smaller wolf form, one which would be more maneuverable and do less damage to her clothing.

If I can do that, she thought, *I can do other things, too.*

She changed into a wolf, forcing the process to happen in the space of a heartbeat, leapt with augmented speed, changed back, then shifted again.

Madame Pataky spun in a circle, seeking a target. She tried simply blanketing the whole area around her with flames, but Bailey jumped over them, and rather than give her position away with a localized shield, summoned freezing rain to descend on the same broad swath of street.

The werewitch was back in motion, cloaking herself, moving at incredible speed, and shifting back and forth as rapidly as she could. The Hungarian's head whipped around in confusion and rising fear. It was as though she were being assaulted by an entire pack of phantom werewolves, their images flashing around her.

"Stop," she grated. "No! Stand and fight."

"Like you stood," Bailey remarked, throwing her voice so it ricocheted around the street, "*behind* all the people you tricked into fighting for you?"

Snarling with wrath, the Hungarian drew a bead on one of the flashing lupine shapes and launched another accelerator-beam at it like the one she'd used on Roland, but Bailey had left a shield in front of her and swept around to the witch's side.

Pataky turned to face her just in time to take the wolf's claws clear down her chest. She fell black, bleeding and waving her hands.

"Bailey! Get back!" a man's voice shouted. The werewitch jumped as three arcanoplasm beams struck the Hungarian, two scissoring across her face while a third pierced her midsection. She exploded into a mass of cinders and pale dust, which the breeze scattered across the pavement.

The werewitch turned, breathless, seeking the next foe. None appeared.

The fighting was over. Her werewolves, the Agency, and the people of Greenhearth had been a match for the Venatori, and the remaining witches they'd duped had reconsidered their priorities.

Bailey rushed back in the direction she'd come before she'd confronted Madame Pataky. She could think of only one thing.

A cluster of plainclothes casters, six or seven women and two men, moved in around her. Lycanthropes watching the scene tensed in case they tried anything.

"We're sorry," they pleaded. "We were misled. If we'd known the truth..."

"Yeah," Bailey said in a hurry, pushing past them, "you're forgiven. Just don't do it again." She was sincere, but Roland still lay in the street. One of the Agency's medics had appeared to tend to him, at least.

She reached the wizard's side and knelt by his hip. "Roland. Are you okay? Is he going to make it?"

Roland seemed to alternate between terrifying periods of stillness and sudden writhing spasms of pain. His mouth was bloody, and his eyes foggy and distant. Bailey bit her tongue to keep from screaming.

The medic grimaced. "It's...hard to say. Honestly, he's not looking good."

"No!" Bailey yelled. "Goddammit, *no!*" She couldn't help herself any longer. She put her face against his leg and sobbed, not caring who saw or what they thought.

Someone stepped up behind her and laid a powerful hand on her shoulder. "Bailey. I'm so sorry." It was Fenris.

She looked up at him, teary-eyed. "Is there anything we can do? I don't know much about, uh, healing." She sniffed.

Before the were-god could answer, a green bolt of lightning struck an empty patch of street fifty yards from where the wizard lay. Gasps and shouts of alarm went around, and everyone turned to see what had happened.

Standing in the midst of silvery-green radiance was the goddess Freya. She'd manifested in her divine form in front of a crowd of hundreds, including normal humans.

"*You*," she stated, gazing straight at her relative. Her voice rolled like thunder.

Fenris looked back at her, stood up, and removed his hood, revealing thick, shaggy hair the color of tempered iron. "Yes, Freya. Me. Were you watching this whole time? If so, you would have seen that my protégé went out of her way to *spare* as many of your children as possible."

Half the witches present fell to their knees. It had taken them a moment to register who stood before them.

The goddess strode toward him, people melting away to let her pass, and she and Fenris faced off ten feet apart with the crouching Bailey and the fallen Roland between them. The Agency medic backed slowly away.

"Yes," said Freya, "I saw." She looked upward, her shining eyes going distant, and when she leveled her gaze again, her face had softened.

She glanced around the town. "This battle has ended without our intervention. Our followers took care of things themselves. Therefore, it is permissible that we intervene in a small way."

Fenris nodded. He knelt and returned his hand to Bailey's shoulder. "Do as she says," he instructed. "Everything will be all right."

Hope flared in the werewitch's chest, and she clamped down on leaping to any conclusions, lest she be horribly disappointed. Still...

Freya crouched beside Roland's shoulder and put her hands on his head. He'd almost stopped moving, although his chest still rose and fell. "My poor child," she whispered. She flashed her eyes toward the werewitch.

"We cannot act too directly in your world, but we can channel our power through a mortal. Place your hands over his wound, Bailey." The goddess put her hand on the girl's other shoulder.

Bailey did as she was told. Then light blazed around her, the deep purple from Fenris combining with the bright green from Freya to form a nimbus of pure white as warm, revitalizing energy flowed through her body and into the man she wanted to be with forever.

Bystanders gasped again as Roland's eyes flew open. He sat up, groaning.

"What the hell? I, uh, I feel better. What happened. *Freya?* Oh, man!"

"Lie back down, you fool," the goddess intoned. "You will still need a normal complement of mortal healing arts to fully recover. But we, through Bailey, have pulled you back from the brink."

Fenris smiled. "A one-time occurrence."

The light winked out. Bailey leaned over Roland, frantically clutching his head and shoulders and planting a long, deep kiss on his lips. She separated her mouth from his and leaned her forehead against his brow.

"Yes," he reaffirmed, "I feel *much* better."

Bailey sprang to her feet, ecstatic and grinning openly, as the medic came back to help him onto a stretcher.

"So," the wizard remarked, "it's been nice visiting the outside world for a day, but I really must be getting back to my usual place at the hospital. Feel free to visit me at home any time."

"I will," Bailey promised.

Fenris took her hand. "But first, know this. You are fit to be a full shaman. There are no more hurdles for you to clear. Nothing more you need to prove before you assume the role, which I knew you could handle."

Freya watched them with a cool expression. "I have no objections. She showed compassion for those of my daughters and sons who'd been led astray by the Venatori's wayward motivations. Let today be a lesson to all witchkind—and werekind."

Then she vanished, the emerald bolt ascending once again into the heavens, and was gone.

The Agency debriefed the volunteer witches and processed the ones who'd spurred them on. Townsend smiled in a grim way as his subordinates led a half-dozen Venatori prisoners toward the back of an open truck.

"We captured their second-in-command," he reported. "Madame Chauvin, who presided over a major slaughter of Weres in West Virginia. Much as we'd like to summarily execute her for crimes against humanity—or lycanthropes, close enough—she's more useful to us alive."

He turned to the short, scowling Frenchwoman as she was dragged past. "That's right, Madame, we'll be having a nice long talk soon. Since we're better people than you are, we won't be torturing you, but you'll talk all the same."

Bailey stood doing nothing and rested in place as a semblance of peace and order returned to the town. Her brothers, Gunney, and the sheriff all found and greeted her, proving they were alive. Russell had been involved in some of the fiercest fighting and had taken a couple of nasty burns and bruises to his legs and torso.

"I'll be fine," he rumbled.

If anyone will, it would be him, Bailey mused.

Townsend raised a walkie-talkie to his mouth. "Bring in the refrigerated truck," he ordered.

The vehicle, not a full semi but approximately the size of a large van, rolled into the town center and down the main street, and as it ground to a halt, agents opened the back to pull out half a dozen cases of champagne.

Townsend turned to Bailey, Sheriff Browne, Gunney, Will, and the rest of her posse. "I had the truck on standby. If the Venatori had won, they'd have been able to claim it as the spoils of war. But letting *them* win wasn't on the agenda. Good job."

"Thanks," Bailey quipped as the townsfolk laughed and cheered, joining the agents in popping corks and spraying foam on the street.

The sheriff's mouth tightened beneath his heavy mustache. "Let's not get carried away with the public intoxication," he cautioned. "Though we'll have a slight relaxation of enforcement for, say, the next two hours."

Gunney smiled. "Sounds like a plan. Fruity wine-type stuff ain't usually my thing, but I'll make an exception in this case." He advanced to accept a bottle. People were passing them around and swigging from directly, even though Townsend had also brought flutes in padded crates.

Bailey took a drink, and then Townsend pulled her aside.

"You did good," he stated. "You've got your wolves under better control, and the rest of the town is getting with the program. That stunt you pulled, hopping around the country to defuse potential shit-bombs, might have made all the difference. We'd have fought more witches here this morning otherwise."

She nodded. "Thanks, Agent. Glad you guys could make it also, though half an hour sooner would've been better. Still, I know you've been busy as hell all over the nation trying to stop the war."

"That we have," the agent acceded, and the tiredness showed on his face. "Anyway, I want to increase our level of cooperation going forward. We have no desire to see the Were community destroyed. But once the Agency rescinds these emergency measures, for fuck's sake, tone the level of weekly catastrophes back down to normal, okay?"

The girl's eyes rotated skyward. "Yeah, yeah, like I had anything to do with the current bout of catastrophes. We *told* them we didn't want to fight, but they just had to push it."

Townsend continued talking, perhaps more to himself than to her. "Covering all this up after the fact is going to be an *apocalypse* of paperwork. Untold levels of form-filling, to the point that the sun will turn black, the moon will turn red, and wine will turn back to water. How do we erase the memories of a quarter of the country? What white lies do we tell, either to the public or to the answer boxes on all those official sheets, that can apply to a pair of gods manifesting, an invasion of witches masterminded by a cult in Europe, and a local defense militia consisting of a bunch of werewolves and their redneck buddies in a Podunk town in Oregon? It's the ultimate fustercluck of fuckassery." He shook his head and stared far off into space.

Bailey laughed and put a hand on his shoulder. "You have my sympathy, Townsend. I can barely stand to do my taxes, simple as they are every year. I wish you luck."

"Thanks," the agent muttered.

The celebration proceeded past nightfall, although as darkness came over the town, the werewolves gradually separated from the humans. Fenris had gone around, beckoning them off. He had something special in mind, that was clear to them all.

"Bailey," he announced, "is to become a shaman."

Nods of approval went through the crowd, and many clapped or cheered softly. Almost all the wolves in the northern Oregon Cascades region seemed to be present.

"I shall perform the ceremony to induct her tonight. Only the pack alphas or other shamans are to see it in full. Those of you who are, come with us. The rest, wait here for our return."

Their deity led Bailey, Will, and the other leaders through the forest to a clearing upon a high ridge, where trees surrounded them on all sides but the moon and stars were fully visible. Fenris stood on a boulder, draped in shadows, while he motioned for the werewitch to stand in the center of the glade under the silver light.

The tall man raised his arms toward the moon. "Bailey Nordin, called Nova," he chanted, "you, along with your pack-followers, have passed the trials within the temple of your ancestors. You have shown great courage, wisdom, initiative, ingenuity, and compassion in your dealings, having defended not only your town and valley but also your people from one ocean to the other. You embody the very best that a shaman, a werewitch, and a lycanthrope can be."

She thought it would be inappropriate to bow her head, although she wanted to blush.

"The path before you," Fenris went on, "will not be easy. Already you've suffered much, and times of great trouble are upon us. But thus far, you've shown yourself worthy of whatever challenge might come."

The alphas and elder shamans raised their fists in salute.

Their god continued, "You are not yet High Shaman," he pointed out, "but I continue to believe you will attain that vaunted position. For now, accept from me the rank of Shaman of Greenhearth and all the packs who dwell in the Hearth Valley. You are confirmed, you are endorsed, you are respected. And..."

Here he paused, and the flicker of a mischievous smirk played about his lips, "...you are free from the traditional obligation to marry before your twenty-fifth birthday."

As the spectators moved forward in a circle to clap hands to hers and offer their welcome and congratulations, she closed her eyes and let out a long sigh, accompanied by a nod so deep it was practically a bow.

I'm off the hook, she thought. *Although that doesn't mean I have zero interest in ever getting married.*

Every available high-ranking member of the Venatori Order was present in the ritual hall. Grandmistress Gregorovia, to her chagrin, was not at the head of the column of sorceresses. Instead, she stood off to the side.

She'd had the dream visions, just as the others had. With the evidence of their Order's new leader in front of her, what could she do?

Facing them all, floating above the altar at the back of the chamber, was a woman whose garb differed from theirs and whose skin gave off a subtle magenta-purple glow. She was beautiful in a subtly eerie way, as though she'd been formed according to an idea of perfection that had forgotten to include the warmth of humanity.

"Mistress…Lady," Gregorovia intoned, unsure how to address the being, "we have assembled here in response to your summons. Tell us why you've come, and we shall listen."

The coldly gorgeous face smiled. Her lips were a deep purple, hair and eyes black, and she wore flowing black robes that seemed ancient, as though they would have been old when the Etruscan civilization first arose. She was bedecked in all manner of sparkling gold jewelry.

"Sisters, daughter," the entity spoke, "welcome. I am your goddess. Your true deity, for Freya has weakened and fallen astray. There are more powers in this universe than the families of the Aesir and Vanir."

The voice chilled them all. It sounded somehow like a whisper bubbling up from underwater, yet it was magnified to the point of echoing through the hall, with each word being clearly enunciated.

Gregorovia balked. What was happening here was unprecedented, almost unbelievable, yet she sensed incredible power emanating from the figure above the altar. Power that dwarfed her own.

"My name is Aradia, and I am the primordial lady of witchcraft. Since your younger patron of the Norse gods is blinded by her relation to her brother, Fenris, I shall lead you to war. For it is to total war you must go. The lycanthropes cannot rise above us, and we must crush this woman-child, Bailey Nordin, and foil the schemes of her patron deity. Witchkind must not be perverted nor surpassed."

Although she didn't like being usurped, Gregorovia found herself warming to the idea of following a goddess whose views coincided closely with hers.

"Indeed," Aradia went on, "that is why I created your Order thousands of years ago. You have forgotten me, but I shall forgive you if you will but obey me. What say you, rightful rulers of Earth?"

The Grandmistress swallowed and spoke for them all after only a second's hesitation.

"We will obey."

"Here," said Bailey, waving toward a bar that gave off distinct honky-tonk vibes. "Unless you're gonna insist we go somewhere swanky and hipster-ish."

"Nah." Roland shrugged. Although he'd still need to take it easy for another week, he was out of the hospital—again—and had regained his usual understated swagger. "I've been in Greenhearth long enough to know I'd fit in there better than you'd fit in at a hipster bar."

The werewitch led him through the doors. Within, the place was much as she'd expected, with a wooden dance floor, a mounted elk's head, and neon beer signs.

"Nice place." She nodded approvingly, and they sat on stools at the bar. "My brothers have never been this far, but I might have to bring them sometime."

With a temporary cessation of hostilities in Greenhearth and the town able to get back on its feet without her, she and Roland were finally taking a short vacation. Today was their first day out, and the bar lay on the outskirts of Bend, where they'd be spending their first night. After that, it was onward to either Boise or Reno; they hadn't decided yet.

They sipped beer in relaxed silence for five or six minutes before a trio of good ol' boys approached them.

"Hey," one said to Bailey, ignoring her partner. "Wanna dance? Looks like you could use a man who can show you how."

"Thanks," she replied in a flat tone, "but I got a man already."

Roland said nothing. Although more than capable of handling the situation even while recovering from his injuries, he respected Bailey's independence—not to mention her abilities.

"Um," the guy replied, squinting at the wizard, "you sure? He looks like he weighs less than you do."

The girl turned her face toward him. "Did you just call me fat?" Her tone was sharp enough to contain an implied warning but not quite a threat. It was his chance to laugh it off and wander away. No harm, no foul.

He squandered it. "No. Why the fuck would you think that? Does this asshole call you fat, and that's why you're so insecure?"

His friend shrugged. "Give it up, Ron. That bitch is crazy."

"No shit," Ron concurred.

Bailey slid off the stool. "That's it. I changed my mind." Her voice was louder. "I *do* wanna dance. March that way, my friends. I dance rough, though."

Roland cleared his throat and whispered, "Remember, this isn't Sheriff Browne's turf, so go easy on them."

"Yeah, yeah," she muttered. "Hold my beer."

He accepted the bottle as she and the three men strode over to the open floor. Noticing that it was half-drained, he raised a hand.

"Bartender!" he called. "Another beer for my girlfriend. She's gonna need a cold one in a couple of minutes."

You made it! Here we are at the end of book 5. Thank you so much for reading this far.

I haven't written *Author Notes* for a while, so let me first express my heartfelt wishes that you and yours have made it through 2020 so far unscathed, or only minorly scathed (is that a word?). This the most amazing year I have ever experienced. I hope never to go through anything like it again!

I saw a memo on Facebook nominating a photo of a baseball field near San Francisco with orange skies from the fires in Northern California and cardboard figures in the stands. They said, "I'd like to nominate this photo of cardboard figures watching baseball in a dystopian hellscape for photo of the year." That about sums it up.

I'm lucky, no fires where I am in Oregon. California and much of the West are burning. It's summer, and not much rain this year. 'Nuff said about that.

Things have been quiet here. Empress Josephine has slimmed down over past few months, due to the number of walkies we have gone on. Storm is doing catlike things, but nothing to report on. I still love my red Jeep. Restaurants open and close day by day, so I have been eating at home and not venturing out much since it's not worth driving to town if I can't get my fish tacos with any degree of regularity. Renée is not a happy camper. Hope your favorite foods are treating you better where you live.

I always thank my advance reader team, but I also want to thank the proofreader team, the ones who read my stories after they are edited. They catch the oopses and point out any last-minute dichotomies, and as such, they helped make this book (and every book) its best. Couldn't do it without you, folks! Thanks for having my back.

I hope you enjoyed Bailey's and Boland's further adventures. They will be back. And if you get a moment, drop me a review, please. Those are the lifeblood of any writer. We appreciate you!

Until next time,
Renée

I COULDN'T DO THIS WITHOUT YOU!

Thanks to my early readers, you rock!

Angel LaVey, Dave Hicks, Deb Mader, Debi Sateren,
Diane L. Smith , Dorothy Lloyd , James Caplan, Jeff Goode,
Kerry Mortimer, Veronica Stephan-Miller

The WereWitch Series
Bad Attitude (Book One)
A Bit Aggressive (Book Two)
Too Much Magic (Book Three)
Were War (Book 4)
Were Rages (Book 5)

Coming Soon
God Ender (Book Six)
God Trials (Book Seven)
The Troll Solution (Book Eight)

Callie Hart Series
Thin Ice (Book One)
Cold Blood (Book Two)
Feelings Run Deep (Book Three)